At First A Dream

Dear Dale & Raquel,

You may never quite fully understand how much your lifelong vocation in the field of adoption has changed so many peoples lives in such a wonderful way. Your commitment, devotion, and kind demeanor is why so many families have turned to JFS in their quest for adopting a child. We thank you from the bottom of our hearts for helping us adopt our son Brendan.

Sincerely,
Jan & Jim Pacenka
&
Brendan

At First A Dream

◆

An Adoption Journey

Vic Goguen
With
Jan and Jim Pacenka

iUniverse, Inc.
New York Lincoln Shanghai

At First A Dream
An Adoption Journey

Copyright © 2005 by Vic Goguen

All rights reserved. No part of this book may be used or reproduced by any means, graphic, electronic, or mechanical, including photocopying, recording, taping or by any information storage retrieval system without the written permission of the publisher except in the case of brief quotations embodied in critical articles and reviews.

iUniverse books may be ordered through booksellers or by contacting:

iUniverse
2021 Pine Lake Road, Suite 100
Lincoln, NE 68512
www.iuniverse.com
1-800-Authors (1-800-288-4677)

ISBN-13: 978-0-595-37474-8 (pbk)
ISBN-13: 978-0-595-81867-9 (ebk)
ISBN-10: 0-595-37474-3 (pbk)
ISBN-10: 0-595-81867-6 (ebk)

Printed in the United States of America

Contents

Foreword vii
Introduction ix
CHAPTER 1   Early Autumn, 1993 1
CHAPTER 2   Christmas 1994 6
CHAPTER 3   Summer 1997–Winter 1998 12
CHAPTER 4   Spring/Summer 1998 16
CHAPTER 5   Autumn/Winter 1998 21
CHAPTER 6   Spring/Summer 1999 29
CHAPTER 7   Autumn 1999 35
CHAPTER 8   Spring 2000 40
CHAPTER 9   June 2000 47
CHAPTER 10   July 2000 52
CHAPTER 11   Saturday, July 29, 2000 62
CHAPTER 12   Sunday July 30, 2000 67
CHAPTER 13   Middle of the Night Monday AM, July 31, 2000 74
CHAPTER 14   Early Morning Monday, July 31, 2000 85
CHAPTER 15   Airborne Monday, July 31, 2000 94
CHAPTER 16   Tuesday, August 1, 2000 102

Chapter 17	Wednesday Morning, August 2, 2000	112
Chapter 18	Wednesday Afternoon, August 2, 2000	123
Chapter 19	Wednesday Night, August 2, 2000	132
Chapter 20	Thursday Morning, August 3, 2000	139
Chapter 21	Thursday Afternoon, August 3, 2000	147
Chapter 22	Thursday Night, August 3, 2000	154
Chapter 23	Friday Morning, August 4, 2000	160
Chapter 24	Friday Afternoon, August 4, 2000	173
Chapter 25	Saturday, August 5, 2000	180
Chapter 26	Sunday, August 6, 2000	185
Chapter 27	November 2000	187
Postscript		189

Foreword

I first heard a brief account of Jan and Jim Pacenka's adoption saga in early autumn of 2000. Along with longtime friends Tony and Elaine, my wife Carol and I had been invited for a cookout and special occasion: we were to meet the newest member of the Pacenka family, Brendan, their six-month-old adopted Cambodian son.

The recounting of Jim's frantic five-day dash around the world to bring Brendan home from Cambodia was fascinating and compelling, and like others who heard it, I automatically remarked, "You should write a book!"

For several days after the barbecue, the story captivated me, and I thought about how the entire adoption process could indeed make an interesting book. I proposed the idea via an email to Jan and Jim later that week. We met to discuss it and agreed to the project. They dearly wanted to provide a written chronicle of the adoption story for Brendan to have later in life, and I saw the proposed book as a perfect opportunity to kick off a post-retirement writing career.

I traveled to Jan and Jim's home one night per week throughout the winter and spring of 2001, tape recording interviews with Jan and Jim after the children were in bed and asleep. During the remainder of 2001 and 2002, I wrote and revised the book with helpful input from Jan and Jim and two other astute first readers, my daughter Deidre, and good friend Richard Dill. After early retirement in 2002, I completed the manuscript and began the long, difficult process of trying to obtain a publisher for ***At First A Dream***. Following two years of unsuccessful attempts to sell the book in a market already awash with a surplus of adoption stories, we made a decision to self-publish. The primary goal, after all, was to produce a written chronicle for Brendan.

With the exception of fantasized chapter "introductions" by the children, the story you are about to read is as factual and as accurate as human memory allows. Some liberty has been taken with reconstruction of various conversations, but they reflect Jan and Jim's best recollections. For reasons of privacy, legality, and author discretion, I have used pseudonyms for the birthmothers and some of the other individuals and organizations mentioned in the book.

Writing this story was a labor of love. Hopefully, you too will enjoy the journey.

Vic Goguen
October 2005

Introduction

This is a story about a journey, both figurative and literal…a journey embraced and endured by a man and a woman wanting to share their lives with a child of the universe. It is a story of love, courage, and above all else, perseverance. It is a journey through the maze of modern-day adoption hurdles, one that eventually spans the globe from Massachusetts to Cambodia. It is both a hellish, plodding journey and a bittersweet adventure bordering on the heroic.

As millions of Americans go about their daily routine of enjoying life in the most prosperous civilization known to man, millions of inhabitants of Third World "developing nations" survive one day at a time. As Americans rush to the nearest mall to buy the latest wireless technology, others dream of one day having electricity in their village. As Americans grow more and more obese, others die slowly from starvation. And as millions of Americans spend a fortune trying to win a lottery, millions of others hope to win an immigration visa, or at the very least, hope that their newborn baby will win a life in America through adoption.

The road to adoption is often a lonely, personal journey, and more often than not, a frustrating quest in pursuit of a haunting image of an unseen and unknown child…a hopeful but exhausting search, day after day, week after week, month after month, and often, year after year. This is the story of one such journey, shared with us, by Jan and Jim Pacenka.

1

Early Autumn, 1993

○ ○

My name is Saveth. I have not yet taken my place in the universe. I will be born in Sihanouk Ville, Cambodia, in the year 2000. It is a small poor village. Elsewhere in the world, people are beginning to worry about Y2K and Zero Day. In Sihanouk Ville, people worry about survival, today, tomorrow and every day.

Jim's stride was effortless. Although no longer a serious runner, prior years of training and conditioning had rewarded him with a trim and fit body that most men in their forties would kill for. He eased into his second mile on cruise control with a pace that would carry him around the nine-mile loop in about fifty-five minutes. Arriving back home, he would finish the run breathing easily and feeling energized. He was still a thirty-five year-old man in a forty-six year-old body.

The run led Jim along winding country roads dotted with large homes on spacious lots, all of them set back a discreet distance from the street. In the eight years since Jim and his wife Jan had built their home, they watched with keen interest as construction crews magically cleared densely wooded lots and developers made new homes blossom as quickly as day lilies. But since most of the houses were being built on two acres or more, the area avoided the overcrowding that was becoming all too common in the "cluster developments" of neighboring towns. Here, homeowners enjoyed country living at its best.

Focusing only on the rhythm of the run, Jim lost himself in the peacefulness and quiet warmth of the late afternoon sun. His mind auto-deleted all memories of earlier workday stress and blocked out all thoughts of the coming evening. There was just the sun and the rhythm of the run.

◆   ◆   ◆

As early evening shadows lengthened, Jan and Jim drove silently along the same country roads that had been his jogging route some two hours earlier. But now, there was a world of difference. For Jim, the blissful synchronized cadence of mind, soul and body was replaced with the drone of the Honda's engine and uncomfortable thoughts of the evening ahead. Their destination was a Boston suburb where they would attend an introductory seminar about adoption. The idea was Jan's, and she was curious and optimistic about the evening. Jim wasn't, and he signed on only as a reluctant observer. Love rules.

The country road was still as beautiful as it had been two hours earlier. But now, the trees were silhouettes against the setting sun and splashes of light on treetops highlighted muted patches of colorful early autumn foliage. The scene was a reflection of Jan and Jim's place in time. Although Jan was only in her mid-thirties, Jim had passed the mid-forty mark, which meant that they too were gradually approaching the early autumn of their lives.

Cupid's arrow had taken its time to find them as they enjoyed the freedom of the singles' lifestyle. Jim was thirty-eight and Jan twenty-nine when they married, but they opted to take time to build a home and try to get themselves financially ahead of the game before starting a family. Delayed marriages and delayed families had become something of the norm in the 1990's, but Jan and Jim's mutual decision had not anticipated that pregnancy might become a difficult proposition. And so it was this evening, with the ticking of their biological clocks getting louder and louder with each passing year, they found themselves driving to a seminar about adoption.

It wasn't that Jan and Jim had given up on the idea of giving birth to their own children. It was just that they hadn't yet been able to conceive their first child, and a flyer at work about an adoption seminar had caught Jan's eye. And they both wanted a family. Jan had grown up in a loving environment with four brothers and sisters. Life then, and life now, was about family love and sharing. All the beautiful new homes, new cars and exciting vacations in the world only had meaning if they could be shared with family. And on that count, Jim, also the product of a loving family and a close brotherly bond, was in total agreement. But he wasn't interested in adoption. Not yet, anyway.

Jim turned up the volume of the car radio to try to drown out his thoughts about the evening as he guided his obedient Honda from country roads to the Mass Pike. This night, there would be no need for State Police to clock Jim's speed on the Pike since he drove like a man in no hurry to get anywhere. Without conversation, it was a long slow journey that seemed endless. But they eventually reached the Route 128 beltway and their exit to the seminar site.

Expecting the social service agency hosting the seminar to be located in a modern office building, Jan and Jim were surprised when the address on the flyer led them to an old but elegant Victorian house in a semi-residential neighborhood. They parked the car and entered to find several other couples already there.

The meeting area was a large room that had probably once been a huge living room. It was tastefully decorated with wallpaper and a plush area carpet that served to accent a three-foot border of beautifully preserved old hardwood flooring. All in all, the room had a warmth to it that might not have existed in a barren modern office suite. It was possible to look around this great room and hear hundred-year-old echoes of large family gatherings happily celebrating birthdays and holidays. How appropriate for an adoption seminar. But it was also possible to survey the room and get the feeling that it was better suited as a funeral parlor. So thought Jim.

Jan and Jim quickly took available seats as it became obvious that introductions had already been made and the seminar had begun. The main presenter was a pretty lady in her forties. She was cordial, but in a cold, business-like way. Professional.

She covered several basic topics about the adoption process before focusing on the various types of adoption. She seemed to be pushing for pure "open adoptions" wherein the birth mother and adoptive parents are identified to each other early in the process, and then spend much time building a personal relationship before the birth. In such an open adoption, a birth mother might even move in to live for some time with the adoptive parents. After the adoption, the birth mother might continue the relationship with the adoptive parents for years, visiting her child at will. Jan and Jim had never heard of such an arrangement. Their silent thoughts were identical, "This is not for us. No way."

As the seminar progressed, interaction between the presenter and the attending couples flooded Jan and Jim with feelings of discomfort, and eventually, alienation. The other couples were obviously in advanced stages of the adoption process. They were not here this night for an introductory lecture. They were here to try to pick up additional tips and angles. One wealthy couple was interested in the presenter's opinion of applying through two different adoption agencies at the same time to increase their odds of quickly obtaining their baby of choice. With some applications running upwards of ten to fifteen thousand dollars each, cost was apparently of little concern to the couple.

In spite of quickly concluding that they shared nothing in common with the other couples other than the desire to adopt, Jan and Jim clung to the hope that surely, in the end, they would come away from the seminar with something positive. That hope was mercilessly crushed when the presenter declared that any negative factors in the medical histories of either prospective adoptive parent would in all cases preclude adoption. "And if you are over forty years of age, forget it."

Jan and Jim couldn't exit the building fast enough at the end of the session. They felt sick. Really sick.

"I feel nauseous", Jan said immediately to Jim as they drove away.

"Me too", Jim answered. "They made me want to puke in there. I can't believe that I can't adopt just because I'm over forty. That's ridiculous."

"And I can't adopt just because I suffered a minor form of cancer fifteen years ago?" Jan said in disgust. "That's just not fair".

As they drove home they vented all their pent-up frustration from the seminar. With each passing mile, their initial feelings of alienation and despair turned to anger and outrage. Though their attitudes were poles apart entering the seminar, they were of one mind after. Based on what they had just heard and experienced, it was "to hell with adoption."

And what angered Jim the most was that he'd paid fifty bucks to suffer through that torture. Never again.

2
Christmas 1994

○ ○
My name is Kimberly. I have not yet taken my place in the universe. But I will. Oh, what a wonderful place it will be! In a beautiful home with lots of room for toys, and with a big yard to play with all the friends I will have. And best of all, I will have a mommy and daddy who really, really, really want me.

Another autumn quietly invaded New England. Right on time. Just as it had last year, and just as it would next year. Although the summer had been enjoyable and rewarding, barren trees reminded Jan and Jim that another year had slipped away without leaving them a child to help warm the approaching cold nights of winter. Vivid recollections of spectacular trails they had hiked in the Canadian Rockies during the summer were already beginning to fade away into the dark tunnel of distant memory. Also gone were the many idle hours of summer that Jan loved to fill by gardening and tending to flowers. Long hours that could be filled, a heart that could be fulfilled.

As annuals succumbed to frosty nights and perennials withdrew into themselves to hunker down for the winter, Jan redirected her energy to her work. She immersed herself in the two graduate courses she taught in occupational and environmental health and safety. The classes dovetailed nicely with consulting work she was doing, and both involvements provided sufficient challenge to make life interesting and enjoyable. Best of all, the work provided a pleasurable distraction from a preoccupation with the passage of time.

Past, present and future equate to time, but time is a meaningless concept without events to define it. Nevertheless, we manage to give it precise definitions. An hour yesterday is exactly the same as an hour tomorrow. A year past and a year ahead are both exactly eight thousand seven hundred and sixty hours. But more often than not, a year past seems to have flown by, while a year ahead seems to stretch to forever. When Jan confirmed she was pregnant in November 1994, the year past seemed to be but a blink in time...yet, day by day, it had seemed like an eternity.

Following the unsatisfying and traumatic adoption seminar in metropolitan Boston a year earlier, Jan and Jim had settled back into life's routines. Work, hobbies, recreation, domestic chores, vacations, and family gatherings had filled the hours, days and weeks. Little was said, but each passing day aggravated a quiet frustration. The clock kept ticking. Adoption was no option. Mother Nature had continued to be disinterested in the simple task of fertilizing an egg. Emotionally, it had been not just one year, after all. It had been five. Five long years of anticipation. Long enough now for mixed emotions. Long enough for a feeling of "why did it have to take so long?" But more than anything else, there was elation. At last, they could look forward to becoming a family.

Most dictionaries provide a dozen or so definitions of the word "family". None of those definitions state that a husband and a wife alone constitute a family. But formal definitions were irrelevant to Jan and Jim, because to them, a family meant parents and children. And that was how they wanted to define themselves. Although further discussion of adoption was avoided following the unpleasant metro Boston seminar experience, they never abandoned the idea that somehow they would have a family. It is often said that necessity is the mother of invention. After five years, for Jan and Jim, persistence became the mother of conception.

Surpressing the desire to run out and tell the world, Jan wanted to get past the first trimester to be sure all was well before spreading the news. She and Jim concluded that the approaching Christmas family gatherings would be the perfect time and place to announce their grand surprise. Their Christmas celebrations were an annual "happening", usually with Jan's family on Christmas Eve, and then with Jim's family on Christmas day. At each location, three generations. Aunts and uncles and nieces and nephews. Grandparents and grandchildren. Mothers and fathers. Children. Family. A perfect time of joy and sharing.

As the holidays approached, the sound of Christmas carols tugged at Jan and Jim's hearts. "Frosty the Snowman", "Winter Wonderland" and other happy songs brought joy and cheerful thoughts, inspiring visions of a future Christmas when they would be crawling around on the floor, playing with their very own children. Sure, playing with nieces and nephews had been fun, would still be fun. But playing with one's own child, well that would truly be special.

But along with the happy songs of Christmas came the somber, deeper carols that strike at the inner spirit with melodious but melancholy lyrics accompanied by weeping violins. "Silent Night" does not make a person feel happy. It is a beautiful song and it makes a person want to sing along. But it haunts the soul. And "Away In A Manger" reminds us that life can be lonely and desolate. Christmas music has many moods, many messages. It reminds everyone that there are the fortunate and the unfortunate. It tries to remind everyone that it is better to give than receive. But ultimately, Christmas music is about a birth. It is about family.

Jan and Jim felt every emotion associated with Christmas as they decorated their home and prepared for the holiday, but it was the joy of the season that filled their hearts. Life had already been good to them, but now, at long last, they were going to be blessed with a child. By next summer, they would be a family. They struggled daily to contain their secret. By Christmas Eve, they were ready to explode.

Noise, happy noise, filled every cubic inch of Jan's sister's home. Adult voices engaged in pleasant banter. Children played with toys and squealed with delight. And of course, there was the ever-present background music of Christmas.

The evening was probably half over by the time two necessary factors converged: a brief lull in the commotion and a sufficient level of courage for Jan to make the announcement.

"Hey everyone," Jan blurted, trying to get everyone's attention. "I've got something to tell you. Jim and I are expecting a baby!"

A hush descended on the gathering of relatives like a scripted Hollywood scene. Then just as spontaneously, the room was filled with an outpouring of cheers, congratulatory remarks, the sound of clinking drink glasses, and joyful banter. The rest of the evening was just a blur to Jan and Jim as extra drinks toasted the special occasion and relatives approached them with their personal congratulatory wishes and hugs...and words of wisdom for the parents to be.

As they lay in bed that night, Jan and Jim couldn't help but reflect on some of the private thoughts that Jan's sisters had shared before the end of the evening celebration. All of the relatives had watched the years peel away like the petals of a flower and wondered when, or if, Jan and Jim would have children. Despite being a close-knit family, good old Yankee courtesy and discretion had kept most of them from broaching the subject during passing years. They all had their own theories and speculations. One sister confided that she had concluded that Jan and Jim had simply chosen to remain childless. After all, with no pets, no kids and carefree summer vacations hiking in the American and Canadian Rockies, it did look like "the good life". And another sister half-seriously confessed, "I thought you and Jim decided not to have children of your own because you saw how rambunctious my kids were growing up."

As sleep enveloped them, Jan and Jim silently pondered the contradiction of the simultaneous complexity and simplicity of human interaction. And they wondered, what kinds of reactions would they get the next day from Jim's side of the family?

They awoke to a cold Christmas morning. But the cold did not bring snow, and a glance out the window told them that they and Bing Crosby would have to keep dreaming of a white Christmas for another year. On the plus side, dry roads would make it much easier for travelers to journey around central New England to spend the day with relatives and friends.

Christmas day traffic was busy but nowhere near as hectic as weekday commuter madness, allowing Jan and Jim to make good time getting to Jim's brother's home a few towns away. And soon, they were immersed in the same happy sounds of children at play, of adults talking and laughing, and of Christmas music filling the air in a perfect harmony of life, just as it had the prior evening. Although Jim's family was much smaller than Jan's, the holiday mood and cheer was no less intense, so Jim found himself patiently waiting for an opportune moment to announce the great news. It came when all had taken seats around the expanded dinning table.

His brother Joe's children had insisted on positioning themselves to be seated around their Uncle Jimmy at the table. They loved Jim, because he was the archetypical "fun uncle" found in most every family. Uncle Jimmy was viewed as an adult playmate, a roll around on the floor, "let's play" kind of uncle that every young child idolizes.

When Jim sensed an opening in the general chatter around the table just before the meal was to be served, he addressed his niece and nephews in a voice loud enough to be heard by all.

"Nicole. JoJo. Adam. I've got a question for you. I've got a question I want to ask you." The children looked at their idol quizzically, uncertain about the sudden seriousness in his voice. He smiled at them. "How would you like a little cousin?"

Joe's wife, LuAnn, let out a shriek of joy that must have been heard throughout the neighborhood. As a three-time mother, LuAnn had understood Jan's desire for motherhood and had been silently praying and rooting for Jan and Jim to become parents for five years.

LuAnn's unrestrained screams of joy and near hysteria startled two of her own children, who began crying in total incomprehension of what had seemingly so upset their mother. Pandemonium reigned. Brother Joe just sat in shock at the other end of the table. Jim's elderly father said nothing, but he sat in his wheelchair with the trace of a knowing smile on his lips. Jim's mother looked confused and dazed as she asked, "What just happened? What's going on?" By the time the first round of hugs, kisses and handshakes had passed around the room, she knew.

For Jan and Jim, the weeks of waiting to tell their big secret had finally come to an end. The wait had been worth it. Jan's first weeks of pregnancy were going well and the surprise announcements had added excitement to a joyous holiday. Christmas dinner never tasted more satisfying. And to Jan and Jim, the Christmas theme of birth and family never had more meaning.

3

Summer 1997–Winter 1998

○ ○

My name is Kimberly. I'm two and happy as can be. I've got toys. I've got friends. I've got cousins. And I've got love. I've got everything except a brother or a sister and my mommy and daddy think I should have one. Course, they don't talk to me about it, but I know. I know everything.

The mid-day August sun felt warm and soothing on her back as Jan bent over the flowerbed to attack unwanted weeds. Above her, the trees were quiet and still, but the nonstop chirping of chickadees made Jan feel she was surrounded by tiny, fluffy friends cheering their approval of her garden. The scent of peonies saturated the air around her and the brilliance of their color in the backlit rays of the sun was simply mesmerizing. When finally satisfied with the results of her weeding, Jan sat on a low stone wall and willed herself to be a sensory sponge. She hated to compare her place in time to a TV commercial, but she couldn't shut off the tag line running through her mind about some moments in life being simply priceless.

Fifty paces away, in a shaded and fan-cooled bedroom, Kimberly slept like a precious cherub. It had been a busy morning. There had been all that playing with new birthday toys, the "reading" of new books, and the playful lessons of TV's Sesame Street. Finally, there had been the long walk with mommy after lunch. That had been the energy drainer that had put her away, even though most of the "walk" had been accomplished in the comfort of a stroller.

Jan walked closer to the house and listened intently to the "baby monitor" attempting to detect any sound from the speaker in Kimberly's room. All was quiet. Jan returned to her seat on the stone wall, closed her eyes and took a deep breath. The aroma of the flowers and tilled earth were natural intoxicants and Jan's mind drifted away to a flood of random thoughts. Of Kimberly, of Jim, of beyond.

Unquestionably, Kimberly's arrival had ushered in many lifestyle changes over the past two years. But since they had so much wanted a child, each change and adjustment was seen as a life-enriching experience, even a joy. But in the midst of the new demands and routines, Jan and Jim both clung tenaciously to valued activities, such as regular exercise regimens and individual jogging sessions. However, joint jogging ventures had become walks, with Kimberly either in a child backpack or a stroller. Hiking in the Rockies had given way to hiking through neighboring woodlands, along New England beaches, or in the White Mountains of New Hampshire. But these local hikes with Kimberly seemed every bit as magical and rewarding as those they had enjoyed in the Rockies, just in a different context. Sure life had changed, but it had changed in a wonderful family kind of way.

There was that word again, thought Jan. Family. They were a family now, the three of them. And during the past two years, there had been the possibility of making it four. Among all the wonderful days following Kimberly's birth, there had been one dark occasion, some fourteen months after Kimberly was born, when Jan suffered a miscarriage. Understandably, it had been an upsetting emotional experience for Jan and it triggered a personal "winter of decision" for her and Jim. On many occasions, once Kimberly was in bed, soul-searching discussions became the evening focus.

Jan could hear herself in one of the nighttime discussions; "We should have another child, Jim."

"Why, Jan? Why do we have to? We've got a nice little family now with the three of us. Things are good the way they are."

"But Jim, I don't want Kimberly to be an only child."

"Why not? What's the big deal? She's got plenty of friends and cousins to play with and grow up with. If we do things right we don't have to turn her into some kind of spoiled brat."

"It's not that Jim. It's not just about growing up. It's about later on. Not that we're that old, but think about it. Although we'll both be around until she gets to be an adult, we probably won't be around for a good part of her adult life. Once we're gone, she'll be alone against the world. That stinks. She should have a brother or sister to share holidays with and to visit with from time to time. Otherwise, she'll be a family of one."

"I suppose."

"Maybe we should take another look at adoption."

"Oh no. No, no. We're not going through that again."

"C'mon Jim, let's not be totally closed to the idea because of that one bad seminar. Some of my friends at work have looked into adoption and they've come away with some pretty positive reactions."

"Let's sleep on it."

But sleeping on it sometimes meant a sleepless night of thinking, tossing and turning. Jan began to spend part of her non-work days researching adoption agencies. The problem was that most of the agencies she contacted were "turnoffs". It might be just some little subtle thing that was said, or it might be the tone of voice, or it might be an attitude that came right through the phone. But more often than not, it was a negative reaction to Jan and Jim's age, or sometimes to Jan's brief battle with cancer in her early twenties. Jan kept searching, refusing to accept her discouraging phone contacts as the final word.

It was an unlikely Friday night in February when Jan had the phone conversation that she had been so doggedly pursuing. To this day, Jan cannot explain to anyone, including herself, why she would have been expecting someone to be around to answer the telephone at 6:15pm on a stormy Friday night, but fate often works that way.

Not only did a social worker answer the phone at Jewish Family Services in Framingham, Massachusetts, but that social worker stayed on the line and spoke with Jan for over three-quarters of an hour. While thousands of motorists crawled along a commuter-choked, snow-slicked Route 9, this angel of adoption totally ignored the "hurry up and beat the storm home" mentality. She listened patiently to Jan's situation, and unlike all the others, offered words of hope and encouragement. In her world, neither Jim's age nor Jan's year of chemotherapy at age twenty-one were considered adoption-stoppers. If Jan and Jim were sincere and persevered, they could, they would, adopt.

By the end of the forty-five minute conversation, Jan was so impressed with the attitude and dedication of that social worker, she was convinced that this was the kind of person who could help them adopt…and who might convince a still reluctant Jim to buy into the idea. That chance connection with a dedicated, compassionate soul on a snowy Friday night put Jan into action for the rest of the winter. She devoted much of her spare time researching all aspects of adoption, especially the pros and cons of international verses domestic adoption. Meanwhile, she and Jim continued to have discussions about the subject. By springtime, Jim was starting to be more receptive to the idea, and it would take only one incident to bring full agreement…another miscarriage.

4

Spring/Summer 1998

o o o o o o o o o o o o o o o o o o o o o o o o o o o o o
My name is Saveth. I still have not taken my place in the universe. But my time is coming closer.

By April 1998, Jan had convinced herself that Framingham's Jewish Family Services (JFS) was the agency of choice if she and Jim were to seriously pursue an adoption. Many calls and follow-ups with other agencies throughout the winter had made the decision an easy one. Without exception, the other agencies were less optimistic and less encouraging. Most of them pushed the idea of international adoptions rather than domestic, and most told Jan that adopting a three or four-year-old toddler was much more likely than the possibility of getting an infant…unless it was a special needs infant.

On a comfortably warm and promising spring night, Jan and Jim once again set off from home to attend an adoption seminar. The beauty of that April evening, with its tease of a coming summer, was lost on Jim. He remained the reluctant participant he had been in 1993. However, this time he was slightly more open to the idea, owing largely to Jan's convincing sales pitch about how supportive and optimistic the staff from JFS were in every interaction. Her winning edge of persuasion was a verbal portrait of a lonely Kimberly at some unknown distant time, Kimberly the adult who would be deprived of lifelong "family" ties unless there were additional siblings. And so once again, Jim drove unenthusiastically east on the Mass Pike toward another evening conference about adoption. Once again, love ruled.

Unlike 1993, the location for this seminar was not an old Victorian house in a residential area of a Boston suburb. This session was to be conducted in the downtown Framingham office of Jewish Family Services, conveniently situated in the basement of the Town Hall. Framingham, Massachusetts is a large, sprawling city that refuses to be a city. The residents of Framingham have stubbornly maintained their town charter since 1700, and with a population of 67,000, they proudly lay claim to being the largest town in the United States still governed by town meetings.

Although the JFS offices were pleasant and non-threatening, and though the JFS staff appeared genuinely warm and friendly, Jim's memory of the 1993 seminar made him feel edgy and uncomfortable. It also didn't help that the overwhelming majority of the fifteen or so participants that night were women. But Jim's initial unease was short-lived as the JFS social workers made all the participants feel welcomed and relaxed. The tone of their presentations was totally "customer-focused". Although they painted a realistic picture of the adoption process, they used a steady brush-stroke of optimism. There were no elitist airs of pretense or aloofness. The JFS social workers were down to earth and made each participant feel wanted and respected. And they communicated their desire to work with each participant to achieve a comfort level whereby the prospective adoptive parents felt they were doing the right thing. "This has got to be right for you" was the over-riding theme.

In contrast to their dejection in the 1993 experience, Jan and Jim left the seminar feeling good about JFS and the possibility of pursuing adoption. They also left thinking in terms of a domestic adoption. They came away feeling so optimistic that Jim convinced himself that the whole process might move real fast, maybe taking only six to nine months. Later, years later, he would come to laugh at his naiveté.

Although Jan and Jim came away from the April 1998 seminar with a positive inclination to pursue an adoption, they did not rush immediately into the process. Jan continued her research and they both searched their souls to be sure of commitment. The singular event that propelled them into action in June 1998 was Jan's very early stage miscarriage.

Convinced that further attempts to become pregnant could lead to another miscarriage, Jan convinced Jim that it was time to get serious about the adoption process. He understood when she said to him about the miscarriage, "I just can't go through that again." Jan called Jewish Family Services and made an appointment for a one-on-one session with the social workers. And what was to become a long slow odyssey, often an ordeal, began in that summer of '98.

If it wasn't for the loving and caring skill of the two JFS social workers, that first session could have become another turning point. The social workers, one of whom was an adoptive parent herself, were masters of positive communication who generated a feeling of absolute trust. They were honest and candid and laid out the path ahead in clear and understandable language. They went over the pros and cons of both domestic and international adoptions and painted a real picture of some of the hassles that lay ahead, including costs and paperwork, paperwork, paperwork…and bureaucracy.

They told Jan and Jim about the required "Home Study Program", a series of one-on-one sessions with the social workers that would stretch over a four month period. There would be a couple of joint sessions held in the office, and then individual sessions with both Jan and Jim followed by yet another joint session, but this one in the home. The Home Study was a legal requirement in Massachusetts for all prospective adoptive parents, and although it did not result in being "certified", it did result in an "official" letter indicating completion. Without successful completion of the Home Study, no adoption.

"We're not here to pass judgment," said the social workers over and over during the intensive questioning for the Home Study. But it was difficult for Jan and Jim to understand why there would be such prying, personal questions if someone, somewhere wasn't going to pass judgment. Sounding apologetic, one of the social workers would also say, "This is something I have to do", as she asked the next probing question.

If it wasn't for the respect and trust that Jan and Jim felt for the JFS social workers, coupled with their commitment to go forward with the adoption process, the Home Study experience could easily have become a major turn-off. The series of interviews dug deeply into every aspect of their lives. Responding to questions about hobbies and likes and dislikes was no big deal. But the interviews pried into every corner of their past and present lives: childhood memories, adolescent experiences, religious background, ethnic background, parental upbringing, financial circumstances and resources, the condition of the home. Probably most irritating was the requirement for the individual interviews to test the veracity of what was said in the joint sessions to assess if Jan and Jim were "on the same track". No judgment?

But Home Study was only the first tiny step towards the finish line in the adoption marathon. Concurrent with the Home Study, in August, Jan and Jim began participating in a ten-session JFS Adoption Seminar Series. The monthly sessions were an agency requirement for all prospective adoptive parents using JFS adoption services.

"The best part about the 'group therapy' sessions were the cookies," recalls Jim. "I really didn't enjoy the 'touchy-feely' sessions, even though many of them were very instructive and informative." They were held in a beautiful large conference room in a high-priced Assisted Living complex rented by JFS. The groups were large, numbering fifty or so participants, and many of the attendees appeared to be much older than Jan and Jim. They included a grandfather who had remarried a younger woman, and the couple decided they wanted children of their own. Jim noted that several gray-haired men appeared to be in their fifties, perhaps close to sixty.

Jim derisively referred to the seminars as "group therapy" because participants sat in a large circle and each had to introduce themselves and tell what was going on in their personal adoption process. Shared frustrations. Shared joy. Shared experiences. Bared souls. Jim would admit to himself that much of it was interesting, especially hearing from those who were far along in the process and those who spoke about coming international trips to adopt. Although Jim, like Jan, felt he could relate to participants, he simply wasn't comfortable in the sharing of feelings and experiences. He generally chose to "just kinda sit and listen." On those few occasions when babysitter complications precluded both of them from attending, Jim happily volunteered to stay home with Kimberly so Jan could attend. But he missed the cookies.

The seminars were often enlightening, sometimes startling. To prospective adoptive parents like Jan and Jim who had prepared themselves with general knowledge about the adoption process, there were eye-opening revelations about the scope and personal implications of such concepts as "open adoptions". They learned it was often possible in such adoptions that the adoptive parents not only got very involved with the birth mother, but that parents, brothers and sisters, and even grandparents of the birth mother might also get into the act. Moreover, any or all of them might opt to make post-adoptive home visits, perhaps for years to come. Although such open adoptions presented an opportunity to increase the adoption odds for prospective parents, Jim and Jan decided such arrangements were not for them. They wanted to adopt a child, not an extended family.

And if the Home Study sessions and the monthly "group therapy" sessions weren't enough to test one's commitment to the adoption process, as summer gave way to fall, and fall to winter, Jan and Jim also undertook two more steps: the formal application process, and the creation of the "Family Album". The fun and excitement of the start of the adoption process quickly turned into a journey of tedious endurance. A pleasant jog along country roads was turning into a steeplechase with new challenges around every corner. But they wanted another child, so they lowered their heads into the bureaucratic headwind and pressed each other on in the race.

5

Autumn/Winter 1998

o o o o o o o o o o o o o o o o o o o o o o o o o o o o o
My name is Kimberly. I'm three and I'm free as a bumblebee. At night, my parents have been going to a lot of something they call "meetings". When they're gone, I have my own meetings with my aunt. I think the meetings they go to are to get me a brother. They think I don't know. But I know everything.

"Jim, this is such a struggle," Jan said as she worked on the outline of the "Family Album" that had become her new preoccupation. Jan had willingly taken the primary responsibility for the creation of the album, while Jim played a consulting and technical assistance role.

"You're doing fine," Jim offered in support, "you're doing just fine." But if the truth were known, he was feeling a bit put out by the project too. It wasn't easy to sit down and try to create a marketing brochure about yourself. That's what the family album had to be, a sales pitch from two would-be adoptive parents hoping to convince a birthmother to select them as the parents for her child.

"This whole thing is embarrassing," Jan complained.

"I know, but we've got to do it," Jim replied. "We can do it. It'll just take time."

"But the social worker wants me to make it too sappy," said Jan. "This 'Dear Birthmother' stuff on the front page seems patronizing, but that's what we're supposed to do. The social worker said that other prospective adoptive parents do the same thing. It's supposed to convince the birthmother how we can sympathize and empathize with her situation. I understand all that, but it still sounds patronizing to me."

By early winter, work on the album had already stretched over several weeks with Jan often working on the project from 9:00pm until past midnight, sometimes until 1:00am. At the start of the project, she'd visualized a format that would simply feature a front-page cover with a picture of her and Jim followed by several pages of family pictures and descriptions. But after showing her first draft to the social worker for comments and editing, she and Jim had been sent back to the drawing board to create a second version. They were told they had to make a stronger direct emotional appeal with the album right up front. This would be accomplished by putting a picture of the three of them, Kimberly included, on the cover, and by writing a 'Dear Birthmother' letter under the picture.

Jan took a deep breath and said to Jim, "Okay, let me read this to you then tell me what you think."

"Dear Birthmother:

We are Jan, Jim and Kimberly. Happily married for 14 years, we have a loving relationship with each other and our daughter Kimberly. We are also blessed with a large, caring, and supportive extended family.

We could never quite know how difficult this must be for you, but we respect the courage and strength that has led you to consider this decision. It is a loving gift to your baby, and to the family you chose. We hope this family album will give you some insight into our family and assure you that we could provide a loving and happy home for your baby should you choose adoption."

"Oh God, Jim, this is soooo bad. I feel like I'm writing soap opera script."

"No, no. It's fine. You're doing great. It's exactly the kind of stuff they told us to write. I know it's not the way we'd approach this, but we have to take the social worker's advice. They know what works. C'mon, read the rest of it," Jim said.

"Being parents has brought tremendous joy to our lives! Parenting another child and providing Kimberly with a brother or sister would complete our family! The three of us have so much love that we wish to share with another child!

With Best Wishes,

Jan, Jim and Kimberly"

"That's perfect. Great job," Jim said with enthusiasm, trying to give Jan an encouraging pat on the back. "Everything you said is true. It's just kinda awkward to put it down on paper and send it to a stranger."

"No kidding. But this is just the front page. We've got a long way to go."

"Don't worry, we'll get there. We've got some great photos to put in this thing. We'll try to let them do the talking for us. Remember that old cliché, each picture is worth a thousand words."

Jim's cheerleading effort was a smokescreen for his own misgivings. After seeing some samples of other albums, he wondered if he and Jan would be as appealing to birthmothers as other prospective couples. Sure they had a beautiful middle class home in the country, and sure they had some great photos of family life and travels. But how could they compete with an album showing a beautiful summer chalet set high on a cliff overlooking the ocean? Or one with a photo showing prospective parents lounging on their cabin cruiser? Or another showing a long driveway with a sports car parked in front of a massive house? How could they compete with albums created by professional photographers and printed by commercial artists?

Jim wondered what would be going through the mind of the young teenage girls and older birthmothers as they leafed through the albums. Were they simply looking for rich parents for their baby? Were they looking for a quality of life that they never had? Were they looking for a certain type of person with a certain type of smile? Were they more interested in the prospective adoptive mother than in the father? Would they care about pictures showing big family gatherings or would they simply see a bunch of strangers with smiling faces? What kind of pictures would appeal to them?

Night after night, Jan and Jim sorted through hundreds of photos they had taken in recent years, trying to decide which pictures would connect with that unknown birthmother somewhere out there in America. They took new pictures of themselves playing with Kimberly, and Jan enlisted her sister to come over to the house to take additional pictures of herself and Jim. They eventually settled on some individual and family travel pictures featuring outdoor life, several photos of a smiling, happy Kimberly enjoying a great middle class life with loving parents, some family gathering pictures, and a picture of their beautiful home in its country setting. Picking out the pictures turned out to be the easy part. Trying to decide the arrangement and order of the pictures in the album, and most difficult of all, writing accompanying narratives and captions was what caused Jan to burn the midnight oil.

Slowly, painstakingly, the album came into focus. Following the "Dear Birthmother" cover, the first page showed individual photos of Jan and Jim hiking in spectacular settings in the American and Canadian Rockies. Alongside each picture Jan composed thumbnail sketches, mini resumes that outlined everything about themselves from their occupations to their hobbies and interests, to selected personality traits. In between the narrative descriptions, Jan followed the advice of the social workers to make it sappy by including personal comments about each other:

> "From Jim about Jan: Jan is a warm, bright, and caring person. She always greets everyone with a pleasant smile and a friendly hello. I am blessed to have Jan as my wife because she is a loving mother and a wonderful wife."

> "From Jan about Jim: Jim is a caring, compassionate, and patient man. I am very fortunate to have such a loving and devoted husband who is also a wonderful father. To him, his family always comes first."

Nothing they wrote in the album was untrue, but they felt silly and embarrassed about selling themselves that way. They also portrayed Kimberly as a fun-loving daughter who would make a perfect sister for some other lucky child...which was also true. And then they had to sell themselves as the perfect family, with Jan and Jim as the perfect parents in that perfect family. The first edition had taken a year to create, and by the time the second edition was a finished product, it was a dozen pages long with some twenty photos and accompanying narrative.

Then came the cost of producing the fifteen copies needed for the marketing process. Not only did they have to spend a small fortune getting fifteen reprints of twenty photos, but also the album had to be produced on expensive parchment paper to try to stay with the competition. Ultimately, the cost of the albums amounted to little more than spare change compared to the rest of the adoption expenses, including the cost of hiring an "adoption facilitator".

Like most adoptive parents, Jan and Jim had begun their adoption journey with a rather simple vision of what the process would entail. But as their education progressed through the application process, the Home Study, and the group seminar sessions, they discovered the incredible complexity of the world of adoption. Maybe somewhere in the dim past, it had been a simple process: a loving man and woman reaching out to provide a home and parental love to a child who was being given up by a grateful mother who couldn't care for the child. No more. Not in the new American millennium. Adoption involved local, national and international government agencies, social workers, lawyers, social agencies, private adoption agencies, and "facilitators".

It was at the group sessions where Jan and Jim learned that working solely through Jewish Family Services would give them very limited exposure to adoption potential. The wait for a baby would likely be at least eighteen months, and perhaps much longer. To expedite the process, they learned that prospective adoptive parents hired the services of private adoption lawyers and specialists known as "facilitators". For fees generally ranging from $8,000 to $14,000, the facilitator became your marketing guru and your salesperson.

Jan and Jim were still debating the pros and cons of "investing" in a facilitator when they caught what they thought was a lucky break. They heard about a facilitator who had left her job with one of the better-known adoption facilitation agencies in the country. This facilitator, Shannon, was starting her own business and was willing to take on clients for the reduced fee of $5,000 in order to establish herself and develop a positive reputation for her new business.

The appeal of hiring Shannon went beyond the consideration of reduced cost. Shannon was herself both a birth parent and an adoptive parent. When she talked about parenting and adoption, it wasn't from a theoretical or academic perspective. Beyond her integrity as a mother, she also proposed to work with a very limited number of clients at any one time. Thinking that they would get much more individualized attention, Jan and Jim decided to sign up with Shannon in January 1999.

Before signing a contract with Shannon, Jan and Jim educated themselves about facilitators. They learned that in Shannon's state of residence, and throughout the United States, there was no such thing as a certified or licensed facilitator. Anyone could hang such a shingle on his or her door. Adoption facilitation was considered a private service. As long as it was limited to advertising, education, support and networking activities designed to solicit and match parties interested in adoption, facilitation somehow did not constitute the legal business of being an adoption agency. Only adoption agencies required licensing.

"I want to be sure you understand my role," Shannon said over the phone, going on to confirm much of what the JFS social workers had already told Jan and Jim. "My primary focus is working with the mothers who find themselves with an unplanned pregnancy and who are considering adoption as a solution to their situation. My advertising and networking efforts bring them to me so that I can then introduce them to prospective adoptive parents."

"And just how do we make the connection with the birthmother?" Jan asked.

"When a birthmother expresses interest in you after viewing your album, I'll contact you and give you her phone number. You need to call her right away. She'll be getting calls from more than one prospective parent. In my experience, usually the first one to call the birthmother is the one who gets the baby."

Jan and Jim filled out Shannon's application form and prepared a check for $5,000. This was to be the first of several leaps of faith in the adoption process. Shannon was not much more than a voice on the phone. The contract simply entitled Jan and Jim to twenty-four months of adoption facilitation services with no guarantee that an adoption would result from Shannon's efforts. In fact, Shannon's brochure stated clearly that she was not in the selection business for either the birthmother or for the adoptive client. Her role was to attempt to bring about introductions of the two parties to each other. She was a facilitator. The rest was up to the birthmother and the client, and then up to the client's adoption agency and the adoption lawyer if a deal could be struck.

"Do you think we're really going to get anything for our $5,000?" Jim asked Jan before putting the check in the mail. "Do you think we're doing the right thing?"

"I think so," Jan answered. "You know as well as I what we've heard about the process. I think this is the only way we stand a chance to get a domestic adoption in a reasonable period of time, or maybe ever. We've got to give it a shot."

"But you've got to admit that we're taking a hell of a gamble here. We're sending five grand off to someone we've never met nor will we ever meet. She's thousands of miles from here, just a voice on the phone. We'll never know how much effort she's really making for us out there."

"I know, Jim, I know. But we've been over all of this. She's got terrific references and a great background in adoption. We know she's not a rip-off artist. The only gamble is how good she'll be working on her own instead of for an established agency."

"Okay, okay. The check's going out today."

As they lay silently in bed that night, both Jan and Jim wondered if they'd made the right move. They told themselves they had. They wondered how long it would be before the phone would ring. What would that first conversation with a birthmother be like? How soon would they find their baby? The stars in the dark sky that cold January night twinkled the answers as they slept.

6

Spring/Summer 1999

○ ○

My name is Saveth. If the choice were mine, I would take my place in the world now. But the stars say I must wait. It will not be much longer, and I will be patient. The planets are aligning themselves in my behalf. Buddha prepares the way.

"I think we're getting ripped off."

"Oh, c'mon Jim, let's try to be fair about this. Let's give her the benefit of a doubt."

"Jan, we've been giving her the benefit of a doubt week after week for months. So far, all we've got to show for our five grand is her 'Quarterly Newsletter' and a monstrous long distance telephone bill for the calls you've been making to her."

"She's just getting her business started, and she's got to get all the advertising and networking channels set up," Jan said, trying to reassure herself as much as Jim. "We should start getting calls from her pretty soon."

Truthfully, Jan was beginning to get as impatient as Jim about the lack of action from Shannon. Each time Jan walked past the phone, she would look at it as if it was part of the problem. It just sat there on the counter, doing nothing. Silent. It was supposed to ring and transmit a voice with exciting news about the possible availability of a baby. *Ring darn it!*

The first call about a prospect finally came in June 1999, some six months after hiring Shannon as their facilitator. She called and left a message on the answering machine that a girl named "Jewel" was interested in Jan and Jim. The message included a phone number for Jewel but provided no other information except that Jewel lived in Nevada and, after seeing their album, she'd expressed an interest in talking with Jan and Jim. As eager as they had been to hear from Shannon, they felt some apprehension about making the first call since there had been very little formal preparation for the birthmother interviews. "We don't want to screw up and say the wrong thing," Jim said as they prepared to make the call. "If we say the wrong thing, the ballgame's over, just like that," he said, snapping his fingers.

"Hello?"

"Hello, is this Jewel?"

"Yes it is. Who's this?"

"This is Jan, and my husband, Jim, is on the extension phone. We were told by Shannon that you were interested in talking with us about making an adoption plan."

Nice going, Jan, Jim thought to himself. Jan got that one right. She remembered that somewhere along the way we were told to never talk about "giving up the baby". That's a no no. Were supposed to use the expression, "making an adoption plan" Jan's on the ball.

"Yes, that's true. I really liked your album."

"Well, thanks. We hope it gave you a good idea about the kind of people we are and the kind of parents we would be for your baby."

And after the first few awkward moments, they talked freely and openly about themselves and their respective life circumstances. Jewel told them honestly that she was living with a guy who was not the father of her child to be. The new boyfriend was an Apache Indian and currently unemployed. "But he's a great guy," Jewel said with pride, "and he wants to be a father when the time is right".

They spoke together for more than an hour on that first call and followed up with several more calls over the next two weeks. Jan and Jim liked Jewel. She sounded sincere to them. The day after the first interview, Shannon had called Jan and Jim to tell them that Jewel told her that she liked Jan and Jim the best of the three couples she'd spoken with. Understandably, it came as a terrible shock, two weeks and several calls later, when Shannon called say that Jewel had decided to keep the baby. Disappointment number one.

Although things didn't work out with Jewel, Jan and Jim felt positive about the experience. At least there had finally been some movement in the process. And the first interaction with a prospective birth mother had taken the edge off the apprehension with the unknown. They'd be more comfortable with the next contact. Moreover, Jewel was likeable and as easy to relate to as any stranger could be over a telephone. They didn't know it then, but Jewel would turn out to be a real "jewel" compared to some of the rough-cut "gems" they would meet over the phone.

Suzanne was the second lead from Shannon. Suzanne had two children from a failed marriage and then she'd become pregnant again with her live-in boyfriend. She said he'd been good to her and her two children until she got pregnant...then he took off to Mexico. Sometime after he left, Suzanne ran into the boyfriend's sister at the local supermarket and discovered from her that he had a family with children of his own in Mexico. Perhaps because Jan and Jim had not been the first couple to contact her, things never really developed past the first telephone interview with Suzanne.

The next opportunity came not from Shannon, their facilitator, but from a Massachusetts private adoption agency which networked with Jewish Family Services in Framingham. The private agency had an available baby from New Jersey that they were unable to place with any of their clients because of ethnicity. The baby was part Irish, part Danish, part English and one eighth Hispanic. It was the one eighth Hispanic factor that supposedly was the problem.

Jan and Jim discussed the ethnicity issue and immediately decided that a one eighth Hispanic factor wasn't really a problem, finding it hard to believe that other couples would. They were interested, especially because the baby was from nearby New Jersey and not some state thousands of miles away. But then Jan and Jim bumped headlong into one of the problems of adoption...money. The private agency wanted a $22,000 "placement fee", and that was on top of another $10,000 in additional fees associated with the adoption. Although they could have managed it, Jan and Jim decided the $32,000 was simply too much money. They passed on "Baby X".

Jan and Jim had learned about the many costs of adoption in the group seminars and from networking with other adoptive parents. One of the expenses they had discovered was the practice of bribing a prospective birth mother. Of course, it was never called that by anyone in the adoption business...but that's what it was, a bribe. In Massachusetts, the legal limit was $1,500. When a relationship was established between prospective parents and a birth mother, it was customary that "expenses" could become part of the relationship during pregnancy. For example, the birth mother might need help with car payments or utility bills or uncovered medical costs during the pregnancy.

Wealthy adoptive parents would circumvent the legal limit in any number of ways to gain favor with the birth mother. For example, in open adoption cases, they might take the birth mother on an all expense paid trip with them to Disney World, or lavish many gifts upon her during the pregnancy. Jan and Jim had decided from the outset that they were not going to play the adoption money game with birth mothers. Nor would they play it with private lawyers. It was common knowledge that if you were willing to dole out $30,000 to $50,000 with some adoption lawyers, they would likely be able to produce a healthy baby of your choice within a relatively short waiting period. Jan and Jim accepted the reality that it would end up costing them thousands of dollars to adopt any baby, but they were not going to go shopping in the upscale baby market.

During the summer of '99, more and more calls came from Shannon. Many of the calls were simply to inquire if Jan and Jim might be interested in one pregnant girl or another. There would be the briefest of information about the prospective birth mother and her circumstances. Usually the birth mother was alleged to be five or six months pregnant. Then, later on Shannon would call back to say the birth mother had decided to keep the baby. Jim again began to wonder if Shannon was simply feeding them false leads to make it look like she was actually doing something in their behalf.

Then there were the pressure calls that also went nowhere. One such call came from Shannon one afternoon in July. She called Jan and told her that a birth mother named Meryl wished to talk with her.

"You've got to call her right now," Shannon told Jan. "She needs $800 rent money for tomorrow."

"Well, that can't work," Jan replied. "You know we work through our agency and our social worker has to check the situation out before we make contact."

"You'll lose the opportunity for this one if you don't call her right away," Shannon insisted. "Some other client will ship her the $800."

"How about if I call her tonight?" Jan said, trying to buy time so she could talk to Jim at work for his opinion…and call the social worker for hers.

"That won't work. It'll be too late. You've got to call her right now."

Jan finally agreed and made the call to Meryl. Any attempts Jan made to engage Meryl in general conversation to learn something about her and her circumstances went nowhere. Meryl wanted to talk only about the $800, demanding that Jan wire the money to her by the next day. Jan tried to diplomatically tell Meryl that she'd first need to consult with her social worker before doing anything about the $800 request. Hearing that, Meryl quickly ended the conversation. So much for that hot lead.

By the end of the summer, Jan and Jim began to question their decision to pursue a domestic adoption. The more they were told about prospective birth mothers, and the more they spoke to them, the more incredulous they became about the "real world out there". Neither Jan nor Jim had grown up in a protective environment, and they knew about the hard side of life, but the passing parade of prospective birth mothers and their life circumstances began to make Jan and Jim feel they had stepped into the middle of a Hollywood mini-series about deviant pregnancies. It seemed like there was no such thing as a normal adoption possibility. Every prospective birth mother they encountered was a hard luck case. Some had been married in the past but were always living with a boyfriend when the unwanted pregnancy happened. When an occasional exception came along, the married birth mother was usually a rape victim. Many of the birth mothers had drug problems, or had boyfriends with drug or alcohol problems. And of course, the alleged loving boyfriends were always great guys when they were straight or sober. All of them had money problems. A few of them seemed to be using pregnancy and adoption as a "home industry" of sorts, getting pregnant again and again within a few weeks of giving up a baby for adoption. They all seemed to be leading totally miserable, dead-end lives.

Each adoption opportunity seemed to turn into a challenge in which Jan and Jim had to make soul-searching decisions about their comfort level with risk-taking. They continually had to decide if they were willing to take a chance on unknown genes, potentially drug-altered genes, or violence-generated genes. Having read much material about the negative effects of drug use during pregnancy, that was their biggest issue…and the one that Shannon refused to understand. But the potential adoption that brought them the most agonizing days and nights was none of those. It was double trouble. Twins.

7

Autumn 1999

○ ○

My name is Saveth. I am alive now, but I am not yet born. My birth mother does not know it, but it is written in the stars that the life she will give me will be nurtured thousands of miles away from Cambodia. I will be a child of the universe...a lucky child of the universe.

In late summer, Shannon called Jan about a new strategy.

"Jan, I'd like to propose something to you and Jim. As you know, each state has its own laws relating to adoption and adoption facilitators. I think we're missing opportunities in Texas because I can't advertise there as a facilitator."

"Oh? So what are you suggesting, that Jim and I advertise?"

"Exactly."

"You're kidding."

"No, not at all. I know the idea takes some getting use to, but believe me, many adoptive couples are doing it. You may be missing an opportunity."

"We'll, tell me about it."

"It's pretty simple. It's nothing more than putting an ad in the personals section of newspapers. I can help you out. You place the ad and I'll reimburse the cost to you since it would be part of the marketing I'd be doing for you if I could place the ad legally."

Jan talked over the new strategy with Jim that night and they decided they had nothing to lose by trying it out. But if they were uncomfortable about the concept of selling themselves as parents with their family album, they were doubly embarrassed about selling themselves with a personal ad in the classifieds of a newspaper. They were thankful the ads would appear in newspapers thousands of miles away so none of their friends and relatives would see them. Nevertheless, they were glad they had swallowed their pride and accepted Shannon's advice when the ads quickly brought a response.

"I've got a prospect for you," Shannon said in a call not long after placing the ads. Jan detected a bit of hesitation in Shannon's voice. After a bit of small talk, she finally told Jan that there was one special angle in the case. "Bonnie", the young prospective mother, was expecting twins.

◆ ◆ ◆

"No way," was Jim's immediate reaction to the news. "Twins? Get serious. We don't need twins."

"Let's at least think about it a little bit," Jan pleaded. "I told Shannon we'd need the weekend to talk it over and make a decision."

"Forget it, Jan. You know as well as I that adoption is a roll of the dice. You want to go for snake eyes?"

They spent all weekend discussing the issue. During the past year, they had seriously discussed all aspects of adoption, from race and ethnicity to the special consequences of rape victim babies. But they had never entertained the idea of twins.

Jan spoke with a friend who had twins and got an earful about the challenges and joys of twins. She spoke with one of their social workers who gave her the name of an adoptive mother who had taken on twins. That lead proved to be a mistake since the bottom line recommendation of that adoptive mother was, "Don't do it!" Meanwhile, Shannon kept calling Jan all weekend to put pressure on her to contact the prospective birth mother. Worn down by the weekend's exhausting discussions and calls, Jim finally agreed to let Jan pursue the possibility. Jan put in the call to Bonnie.

Conversation with the young expectant mother flowed easily from the very first call. Bonnie seemed socially awkward or backward, but she liked to talk. She told Jan and Jim that she had two sons from a previous marriage. She said she was four or five months pregnant and the father was a boyfriend who was currently in jail for non-support of three boys from his failed marriage. She'd been forced to move back in with her parents after her own marriage broke up.

Bonnie said she was part Indian but was not registered with the tribe so that wouldn't be a factor in planning an adoption and no permission would be needed from the tribal council. Jan was relieved to hear this because one of the summer's fizzled adoption possibilities had resulted from technicalities with the birth mother being a registered Indian on a reservation.

After a few telephone conversations, Bonnie told Shannon that she liked Jan and Jim and wanted them to be the parents of her expected twins. This news suited Jan and Jim because they too were taking a liking to Bonnie. The long distance telephone relationship grew stronger with every call. Even three-year-old Kimberly went around telling everyone in sight, "We're adopting twins, you know!" These declarations to strangers in line at the grocery store, or anywhere else, brought smiles to many faces but a touch of self-conscious embarrassment to Jan and Jim. They soon began to wish that they hadn't sat down to inform their precocious daughter about the adoption process.

Most weeks, Jan and Bonnie would have a one-hour conversation about anything and everything. Bonnie talked about her job as a nurse's aide at a local hospital and about her leisure activities. Even though Jan couldn't identify with everything about Bonnie—whose idea of a big night out was local dirt track car racing—the young mother was likeable and engaging over the phone and seemed to be a more desirable candidate than some of the other contacts that Jan and Jim had experienced during the summer. So Jan and Bonnie would talk and talk, and soon the subject of initiating adoption paperwork came up with an agreement that Bonnie would complete some forms that Shannon would forward to her.

Weeks went by and Bonnie never quite got around to completing the paperwork for Shannon, nor did she get around to sending pictures of herself that she had offered to send. But she still loved to talk with Jan like a long, lost friend. She began to suggest that Jan and Jim should come down to visit with her, maybe even accompany her to an ultrasound test. At the time, such a visit wasn't really an option for Jan and Jim, and they were starting to cool a bit in the relationship due to Bonnie's excuses for not getting the paperwork done…especially after two months.

When Jan began to express concern about the situation, Shannon chastised Jan with a flip, "you're worrying too much" response.

"Do you think I'm worrying too much?" Jan asked Jim.

"If you ask me, we're not worrying enough. Why won't Bonnie do the paperwork? Something doesn't feel right. If she likes us and want us to be the parents, why would she keep us hanging two months?"

"I agree, and something else doesn't make sense. In last night's conversation, she told me that the doctor said her babies were now four pounds each. There's no way her babies can be four pounds each when she's only four or five months along."

"I think it's time to bypass Shannon and try to get a handle on what's going on," Jim said. "As long as were committed to this situation, Shannon isn't going to come up with any other leads. So if things go nowhere with Bonnie, we've just wasted three months."

After consulting with their JFS social worker, Jan was further convinced that something was amiss in the Bonnie situation. A plan was developed to hire a Texas social worker to pay a "routine" visit to Bonnie to assess the circumstances of the pregnancy and life situation. The social worker called Bonnie to make an appointment and went out to visit her. When the social worker arrived for the designated appointment, Bonnie wasn't home. It was unclear from Bonnie's mother where Bonnie was or when she'd return home. The social worker took a room at a local motel and returned to Bonnie's home the next day. No Bonnie. Subsequent attempts by Jan to reach Bonnie by telephone were unsuccessful.

After discussions of Bonnie with Shannon, there were only theories about what had gone wrong after months of relationship building. One possibility, based on the unrealistic claim by Bonnie that her twins each weighed more than four pounds each by the fifth month of pregnancy, was that Bonnie was not even pregnant and was one of many young ladies who attempt to scam prospective adoptive parents. Another possibility according to Shannon was that Bonnie's boyfriend talked her into getting involved with a laywer-facilitator who could deliver prospective parents willing to pay big money for the twins, possibly dangling the potential of $5,000 per twin in front of Bonnie. The lawyer, of course, would make even more. The downturn in Jan and Jim's relationship with Bonnie seemed to have begun just about the time Bonnie's boyfriend was released from jail.

Jan and Jim were crushed. Not only was there a depressing letdown from what had been such a promising relationship, but also there was the frustrating reality that several months had been wasted. How many other leads might have been more fruitful? They would never know. Moreover, birthmothers typically shy away from making any adoption plans during the holiday season, so it might be late January or February before Jan and Jim received any more leads. And to add to their emotional devastation, Jan and Jim had to try to cheer up a very disappointed little Kimberly who could no longer keep telling the world, "We're going to have twins, you know". Over and over she would ask Jan why the twins weren't coming. Over and over Jan would simply answer, "Bonnie decided to keep the babies".

Although another Thanksgiving holiday brought many things to be grateful for, the adoption process was not one of them.

8

Spring 2000

o o o o o o o o o o o o o o o o o o o o o o o o o o o o
My name is Saveth. My Cambodian mother abandoned me the day after I was born. She has done this so that I may have a better life than she can provide. A surrogate mother will care for me until I can be sent to the orphanage. Buddha watches over me.

It is past midnight, and though their eyes are closed, both Jan and Jim lay silently awake…frustration their bedmate. A late-night e-mail from Shannon has effectively assured another restless night. Following the disappointing end to the Bonnie affair, little or no communication came from Shannon during the winter holiday months. Shannon had pretty much stopped calling Jan. Her new approach took the form of late-night e-mails. She, of course, was sending them during mid-evening, but due to the West coast to East coast time difference, Jan and Jim would usually receive the e-mail around 11:00 to 11:30 pm.

Shannon's late night e-mails were never happy bedtime stories. More often than not, she would be inquiring or following-up about their interest in a problematic and likely undesirable potential adoption. For example, even though Jan and Jim had stated in their application with Shannon that they were not interested in adoptions with birth mothers who were drug addicts, Shannon would still send e-mails trying to interest them in such potential adoptions. Out of desperation, Jan once spent a long winter day researching amphetamine drug abuse only to discover the next day that the latest prospective birth mother was actually a cocaine addict. When Jan and Jim rejected the candidate, Shannon admonished them for being "too picky".

Jan and Jim had discussed the option of not checking for e-mail at bedtime, but hope springs eternal, and the gods of possibility beckoned Jan to her computer each night with whispers of temptation. There was always the hope that the next e-mail was the one that would lead to a "happily ever after" adoption. On this Wednesday night, Jan had felt compelled to check for mail since she and Jim were leaving for New Hampshire the next day. They would be away for several days for an annual cross-country skiing vacation with friends and family. But tonight's e-mail was as frustrating as ever. Shannon's message was a brief, uninformative e-mail about an available "rape baby" in Colorado. "If you want this baby, it's yours. Come and get it tomorrow."

Jim was very aggravated with everything about Shannon's communication. It bordered on the absurd. Here she was sending them an urgent e-mail to make a quick decision about adopting a baby without any information other than the pregnancy had resulted from a rape. And with only that information, she expected Jan and Jim to jump on a plane the next day to pick up the baby in Colorado.

"This is getting nuts," Jim fumed before going to bed. "This whole relationship with Shannon is getting reversed. We paid her good money to work for us, and now she treats us like we're at her beck and call. She expects us to jump at anything she sends us."

"I know, I know, but Shannon's still our best hope for getting a baby. We've got to keep working with her. I'll send her an e-mail response telling her we need more information," Jan said patiently. But she went to bed just as emotionally upset as Jim. And both of them lay there silently reviewing their recent conversations about perhaps dumping the whole domestic effort with Shannon and shifting their focus to an international adoption. As their dissatisfaction with Shannon grew, they had started to research Cambodian adoptions and had given some half-serious thought to the idea.

The next morning, before leaving for New Hampshire, Jan called Shannon and learned that the rape baby might not be a rape baby at all. Shannon thought that the young mother fabricated the rape story rather than tell her mother that she got pregnant by a local boy from the high school. Jan told Shannon that she and Jim would be interested. Shannon said she'd call back but didn't.

Jan then spoke to her social worker from Jewish Family Services. She told Jan she would look into the Colorado situation for them while they were in New Hampshire, but had another good prospect for them. The new opportunity was in Boston. A young Vietnamese girl had become pregnant in her relationship with an Irish boyfriend. She was a college student and wanted to stay in college to become a success story in the Vietnamese immigrant family. She was almost due to give birth and had decided to place the baby for adoption. This prospect sounded very promising but Jan told the social worker that the Colorado baby also sounded very promising and stressed that she and Jim wanted to keep both options open. Jan gave the social worker a phone number in New Hampshire where she and Jim could be reached over the long weekend they'd be away. If necessary, Jan and Jim were prepared to cut their vacation short and do whatever was necessary to make the potential adoption of the Irish/Vietnamese baby move forward...or fly to Colorado to pick up that baby.

◆ ◆ ◆

Jim leaned slightly into the wind as his strong legs pushed in perfect synchronization against his cross-country skis, propelling him in a swift glide over the sparkling fresh snow. Jim was usually "the rabbit" on these trail runs. A bit younger and in better physical condition than his friends, he'd frequently zoom ahead a hundred yards or so around the next bend in the trail, then wait for everyone to catch up. He was the scout, making sure all were forewarned about a steep drop or dangerous curve ahead.

This early March skiing weekend with friends at Waterville Valley had been an annual event for many years. Kimberly's arrival on the scene had not changed the get-together, only the arrangements. Jan and Jim took turns each day with the babysitting duties, each getting in trail time with the other couples. Dining out simply meant adding a baby chair to the table. As Kimberly grew older, she became part of the "entertainment" at the gatherings.

The adoption process was much on Jim's mind as he schussed along Drake Brook's Trail. From the start, he had been a reluctant participant, allowing Jan to drive the process. He was committed to it, but he was not overly enthusiastic. As it became more and more of an ordeal, his motivation became driven by pragmatism. He just wanted to get the deal done. It was that desire for a conclusion that was getting him to think more and more about an international adoption. From what he and Jan had heard, the international route would be a quicker, surer bet for positive results.

As Jim reached the crest of the trail that marked the start of the run down to "Hairpin Turn", he stopped to wait for the rest of the group who were huffing and puffing a herringbone duck walk up the steep hill. Lost in thought, he smiled to himself as he ran a mental video of last night's social hour after Kimberly had gone to bed. The group of friends knew about Jan and Jim's interest in adoption. Conversation had naturally drifted into the latest developments, especially Jan and Jim's anticipation of a call over the weekend about the latest prospects in Boston and Colorado. Jim mentioned in passing that if there wasn't success soon in getting a domestic adoption, he and Jan might seriously pursue an international adoption, perhaps in Cambodia. That comment brought instant, candid reaction from one of the friends.

"Cambodia," Tony blurted in disbelief. "Oh, come on! You're gonna go get a kid in Cambodia? Cambodia! What do you want to do that for? You've got beautiful little Kimberly. The three of you make a nice family. Why do you want to go running off to Cambodia to get another kid?" And before either Jim or Jan could attempt to give an answer, Tony turned to his wife, and pleaded, "Elaine, can't you help these guys?"

Jim looked down the trail at Tony and the others laboring up the steep hill. He smiled again thinking about last night. He wasn't upset with Tony's reaction. It was an honest reaction from a traditionalist…and an old friend. Jim supposed it could be hard for people who took normal pregnancies for granted to fully understand the motivation of couples desiring to adopt. Jim thought briefly about Cambodia. Then he thought about the hopeful call about the Boston Vietnamese baby. Then he pushed off confidently toward The Hairpin.

◆ ◆ ◆

Disappointingly, there were no developments during the weekend at Waterville. Upon return, Jan was shocked to learn that while she and Jim were in New Hampshire waiting for a call, Shannon had consulted with one of the JFS social workers and the two of them had arbitrarily decided that the Boston prospect was best for Jan and Jim. Shannon, who was given full decision power by the Colorado birthmother, then placed the baby with another couple when the baby was born during the weekend. Jan and Jim were furious about the lost opportunity that had been taken away from them and had no choice but to pursue the Boston possibility with greater than ever intensity. A flurry of calls to the JFS social worker resulted in a plan for Jan and Jim to meet the birthmother on Friday of that week. But before Friday could arrive, the birthmother went in for an early delivery. However, she let it be known that she wanted Jan and Jim to have the baby and requested that they use Michael or Jacob as a first or middle name.

◆ ◆ ◆

"How about this one?" Jim inquired hopefully, proudly holding up his selection. Jan looked at the pretty blue baby outfit and nodded her agreement. Jan and Jim were borderline ecstatic the entire weekend. Much of the time was spent on a shopping spree for the baby they were to bring home by Tuesday. They were giddy with joy as they cruised up and down the aisles of Spag's, a legendary discount store that was like a huge warehouse-sized country store. By the time they reached the cashier, they were loaded down with more than $400 of clothes, diapers, bottles and nipples, a changing table and other necessities for their new baby. They even bought a heart-shaped gold locket to give the birthmother so that she could have it to hold a picture of her baby. Exhausted by their shopping and elated with their preparations for the baby, they enjoyed sound, peaceful sleep. They never could have dreamt what Monday would bring.

♦ ♦ ♦

"No! I can't believe this!" Jan exclaimed, fighting tears. Jim watched helplessly as Jan pleaded with the social worker over the phone. "I can't believe this! Can't you get her to reconsider? Maybe if she thinks more about it for a day or two?"

"I'm sorry, Jan," said the social worker. "I'll try, but usually if a birth mother has any reluctance at all about giving up the baby during the first few hours after birth...well, she usually doesn't give it up."

"I can't believe this! Please try."

Jim was jumping out of his skin with eagerness to hear what had gone wrong, but he had to give Jan a minute to compose herself as she slumped into a chair, her face grief-stricken.

"We probably won't get the baby," she said in a despondent whisper. "I can't believe this. The birthmother's father has gotten into the act and the whole adoption is down the tubes."

Slowly, painfully, Jan recounted the story she'd gotten from an equally disappointed social worker. Apparently, the birthmother and her mother had kept the pregnancy secret from the birthmother's father. The father, who was now a thirty-seven-year-old grandfather, could not accept the disgrace of his unmarried daughter giving birth to a child. When the mother attempted to stand by the daughter, the father had flown into a rage and told the mother to choose between him and the daughter. Unable to abandon her daughter in this time of emotional need, the mother said she would stick by the daughter. The father left. The birthmother, now feeling guilty that her pregnancy had broken up her parents' marriage, decided that keeping the baby would give meaning to the pregnancy. She would raise the child with the help of her mother.

It took a day for Jan to run around to Spag's and several other stores to return all the purchases. That reality check and an email from Shannon about a birthmother in California wanting $15,000 made for an Easter weekend short on joy and rejoicing. Jan fired off an email response to Shannon informing her that a payment of that type to a birthmother violated Massachusetts law and then when on to express great displeasure with Shannon's arbitrary decision-making in denying them the opportunity for the Colorado "rape baby". When a suggestion was made by the JFS social worker the following week to "get off the merry-go-round and go for the brass ring," Jan and Jim decided it was time to go international. It was the only way to resurrect their hope for adoption.

9

June 2000

o o o o o o o o o o o o o o o o o o o o o o o o o o o o o

My name is Kimberly. Pretty soon I'm going to have a birthday. I'm really getting old, you know. I'm going to be five. That's old.

Jan sat on the stone wall of her flower garden, admiring the results of an hour's weeding and cultivating. It always amazed her to see how the early summer sun could make perennials rocket out of the ground by simply warming the moist soil. Something…no…everything about nature's annual resurrection was fuel for the soul. Symbolically and prophetically, the circumstances of Easter weekend had led her and Jim to decide to go international, injecting new life into their adoption hopes and dreams.

Deciding to keep all options open, and wanting to get as much mileage as they could for their $5,000 investment, they had started to pursue the international route as a parallel effort, without informing Shannon. Assuming that the odds of effecting a domestic adoption through Shannon's efforts were slim to none, they began actively researching international adoptions in April. After intensive research, including discussions with parents who had gone the international route, and after consultations with their JFS social workers, Jan and Jim narrowed the choice to three countries: Cambodia, Guatemala and Romania. Each had their advantages and disadvantages, but thousands of successful adoptions seemed to point to Cambodia as the country with the most promise.

The social workers at JFS pointed Jan and Jim towards the Maine Adoption Placement Service (MAPS), a non-profit organization specializing in international adoptions. MAPS had a very credible track record and worked in cooperation with West Coast International Adoptions Agency (WCIAA), an agency that specialized in facilitating Cambodian adoptions. But as Jan and Jim were quick to discover, the international adoption application process was every bit as bureaucratic and tedious as was the domestic route. Thankfully, Jan and Jim found the MAPS social workers eager to help with the mounds of paperwork.

Jan and Jim worked as a relay team for almost two months to complete the required paperwork, which essentially was a duplicative effort that produced an application package for MAPS and a "dossier" for the Cambodian adoption bureaucracy. Jim's role was to run around obtaining needed documents while Jan completed required forms and assembled the packages.

The breadth and depth of documentation was exhausting. The usual credentials such as birth certificates, marriage certificates and passports were only the beginning. Above and beyond medical history forms and proof of health insurance, a testimonial letter from the family doctor was also needed. Besides three character reference letters, they had to get a letter from the local police department. Along with tax returns, all manner of financial records were needed to establish complete asset and liability documentation.

They also needed to complete the "Cambodia Home Study Outline", provide a family album, obtain various powers of attorney, write letters to several Cambodian Ministries involved in the international adoption process, sign a post-placement agreement to submit photos and reports about the adopted child, and sign a health waiver for the proposed adoption which essentially said that the baby came "as is" without any warranties. And everything submitted in the application and dossier packages required notarization and duplication to the tune of eight copies…all of which Jan and Jim had completed by the beginning of May.

◆ ◆ ◆

"You're kidding," Jim said, "already?"

"Yes," Jan beamed, "isn't this incredible?"

"How long's it been since we sent the stuff in? Can't be more than a couple weeks."

"That's about it. Really, they don't mess around," Jan agreed. "I asked them to fax the info they had about the baby to my brother so we'll have it when we get back home."

"What did you say the baby's name was?"

"Saveth."

"How old?"

"Just a few weeks. MAPS said he was born on March 28th and abandoned one day later."

"This is fantastic, Jan. We should've done this long ago. We pay Shannon five thousand bucks and get nothing but aggravation for a year. We pay MAPS nine hundred bucks and WCIAA gets a Cambodian baby for us in less than a month!"

Jan and Jim continued to excitedly discuss the call that they'd just received from West Coast International while Kimberly watched TV with friends in an adjacent hotel room. The family was in Florida. They had taken the opportunity to turn a work-related conference Jan was attending into a mini-vacation at Disney World. Jan had given MAPS their hotel phone number in case there were some developments while they were in Florida.

Although they enjoyed their brief vacation at Disney, Jan and Jim anxiously returned home to begin reviewing the information that had been faxed by MAPS. As luck would have it, another international adoption possibility, a baby named Bun Lee, was forwarded to Jan and Jim by West Coast International. Pictures of the babies were forwarded over the Internet. Jan and Jim were elated to have real adoption possibilities before them, but they felt it bordered on the bizarre to be choosing a son from pictures on a computer. But then again they thought, wasn't it wonderful how Internet communications could speed up the slow, cumbersome process of adoption? They had no idea just how dizzying the pace would become by mid-June.

♦   ♦   ♦

Since there were some serious medical issues with Bun Lee, Jan and Jim decided to pursue the adoption of Saveth, but that decision was not without some of its own medical concerns. Jan had consulted Kimberly's pediatrician with the information first made available by MAPS. The pediatrician was not comfortable with Saveth's body size. The baby weighed only five pounds, six ounces at five weeks of age, and the doctor was especially concerned about the size of the head. MAPS assured Jan and Jim that the baby's health was quite good, but they agreed to get additional data. A doctor associated with MAPS, Dr. Nancy Hendrie, who traveled to Cambodia on a monthly basis to check on the health of the babies, would get more up-to-date information about Saveth on the next visit, scheduled for June 12th. The conclusion: Kimberly's pediatrician was applying American standards to Asian babies. The circumference of Saveth's head was well within the normal range for Asian babies.

Jan felt great relief when the medical concern was resolved. She and Jim experienced a good feeling every time they looked at Saveth's picture. He was going to be "the one". They were sure of it.

♦   ♦   ♦

"What do you mean there's going to be a moratorium?" Jim blurted.

"Just what I said, Jim," Jan answered, trying to stay calm. "It's all very confusing, but there's a big to-do brewing about Cambodian adoptions. There are all sorts of rumors but it seems like internal political battles between the different Cambodian ministries are messing things up and there has to be a revamping of the whole adoption process. The US State Department and the Immigration Department are declaring a moratorium on American adoptions from Cambodia until things get squared away."

"You've got to be kidding! Can this be for real? What can we do?"

"We've got to finalize everything right away. West Coast International says the moratorium takes effect on June 15^{th,} but if we get everything officially in process before the shutdown, our adoption can still go through."

"Let's do it."

And they did, though it was June 16th before the acceptance paperwork was faxed to West Coast International along with a wire for the $2,500 acceptance fee. Additionally, Jan and Jim wired $5,500 to the Cambodian Ministries, a sum required for the "processing" of the adoption. Their heads spinning from the flurry of activity, Jan and Jim wondered if they might be headed toward another disappointment…an expensive one at that…in their quest for an adoption. West Coast International assured them that the adoption would go through because of verbal agreements made on June 12th after Saveth's medical examination by Dr. Hendrie.

The second half of June did nothing to build confidence. One of Jan's friends, who also had pursued an adoption from Cambodia, learned that her scheduled June trip to Cambodia to pick up her baby had been cancelled. There was much confusion about the moratorium. Rumors about fraudulent Cambodian adoptions and baby trafficking surfaced daily and spread quickly through Internet bulletin boards and chat rooms. Since solid, factual information was non-existent, Jan and Jim put their faith in the known integrity and credibility of MAPS. As the 4th of July approached, Jan and Jim wished they had a crystal ball so they could peer into the future to see if Saveth would some day be standing at their side, waving a small American flag as the parade marched by.

10

July 2000

○ ○

My name is Kimberly. Pretty soon I'm going to be five years old…and…I'm gonna have a brother. My Daddy told me. His name is gonna be Brendan Saveth Pacenka. Daddy showed me his picture. He's so cute. It's gonna be so fun to have a baby brother.

The international adoption roller coaster ride continued throughout July, taking Jan and Jim on rushes of exhilaration and heart-stopping dives. They were elated when West Coast International told them that their paperwork had successfully run the gauntlet of all five Cambodian Ministries involved in the adoption process. They had been concerned about this phase since they'd heard that one of the five Ministers had taken a dislike to the expansion of American adoptions and had been quoted as saying something like, "I'd rather see these babies suffocate than go to these American Capitalist Pigs". Apparently, the $5500 Cambodian Government processing fee for each adoption helped him to suppress his hostility long enough to sign-off.

But no sooner had Jan and Jim sighed a relief that the road ahead was clear, they learned that Cambodia had put international adoptions on hold again. West Coast International organized a letter-writing campaign to the Ministries and provided letter formats for prospective adoptive parents to use in their pleas to the Cambodian Government. WCIAA also sent a representative to Cambodia to attempt to facilitate the process. Just as it appeared that the adoptions were back on track,

Jan and Jim learned a week later that all American adoptions were again on hold. The story this time was that the French Government had prevailed on the Cambodians to expedite only the adoptions from France. Finally, on the evening of July 14th, Jim received a call from West Coast International to say everything was a go. Wonder of wonders...July 14th! France's Bastille Day! How providential. Jan and Jim's adoption of Saveth would indeed be part of the last group of American adoptions before the moratorium door slammed shut. WCIAA told Jim to go ahead with planning and booking travel arrangements.

With West Coast's receipt of the official decree, a Certificate of Adoption from the Kingdom of Cambodia, Jim began preparing in earnest for the trip to Cambodia. His initial plan was to attempt to make the journey during the last week in July. Jan and Jim had become friendly with another prospective adoptive couple from a nearby town and they were going to Cambodia at the end of July to pick up their baby, the same week that Jan's co-worker and her husband were going. Jim thought it would be great to be traveling halfway around the world with some friendly faces, but it wasn't meant to be. Saveth's adoption processing in Cambodia could not be done before the first week in August. But it was all for the best because Jan discovered that her friends' travel arrangements were terrible, including an all-day layover in Bangkok. Worse yet, they'd still be arriving in Cambodia several days too early for the group adoption processing, essentially stranding them in Phnom Penh for a few days. With Jim agreeing that he'd rather go it alone than spend several days hanging around a hotel in Bangkok or Phnom Penh, Jan began searching for an alternate travel agency that could produce more desirable arrangements. Ultimately, the plan was for Jim to leave New England on Sunday night, July 30th, arrive in Cambodia on Tuesday, get through the adoption processing, and return Saturday, August 5th with baby Brendan.

Along with travel planning, the last two weeks of July became a marathon of final preparations. A major obstacle had been to sort out the best information in the travel packets that had been provided earlier by both MAPS and West Coast International. The packets, which offered comprehensive instructions on everything from money issues to recommended travel agents to medical considerations, contained several areas of contradictory information, not the least of which pertained to vaccinations and needed medications. Jan had to do much research on the Internet and consult with the family doctor and Board of Health to verify the need for Tetanus, Hepatitis A & B, and Polio shots.

The most vexing question had to do with the need for preventative malaria pills. Taking malaria pills generally causes a person to become quite sick. Nevertheless, most of the advice and research Jan could find highly recommended taking malaria pills before initiating travel to Southeast Asia. The one exception found was for travel to Phnom Penh, so ultimately, Jim opted to gamble and skip the malaria pills.

Jan and Jim also had to become educated about such things as the need for "Scabies Lotion" and other medications, while obtaining extra prescriptions of all types from the family doctor and Kimberly's pediatrician. A skeptical pharmacist asked Jim, "Can you tell me why you need all this medicine?" Jim could, of course, and eventually completed his preparation of what amounted to a small traveling medicine chest as recommended in the travel packets.

Another area of confused instructions revolved around the paperwork required for American bureaucracies, especially the Immigration and Naturalization Service (INS). One of the forms required by the INS was essentially a contract of sorts between the adoptive parents and the United States Government that sought to "guarantee" that the foreign child being brought into the country would never become a financial burden on the U.S. government. The form documented the income sufficiency of the adoptive parents to provide financially for the child and was needed to reenter the United States with the adopted baby. Despite many calls and inquiries, Jan and Jim could never get a suitable answer as to whether Jim would need a Form 684 or a Form 684A. The basic 684 would be based on Jim's income alone, while the

"A" would be based on joint income. Since Jim would be reentering the country alone with the baby, there was a question as to if he'd need the form based solely on his income. Frustrated with their inability to get a clear answer, Jan and Jim completed a set of both Form 684 and Form 684A so Jim would be ready for the INS no matter what they wanted. Of course, not only were multiple copies of both sets of forms required, but also, both had to be notarized. Of course.

◆ ◆ ◆

The issue of bringing Saveth home to America had been a hot item of discussion between Jan and Jim during much of July. They agreed that although it was theoretically possible for both of them to journey to Cambodia, it was impractical and posed double jeopardy for Kimberly. The raison d'etre for the adoption was to have an expanded family and a lifetime brother or sister for Kimberly. If both Jan and Jim made the trip to Cambodia and something tragic happened, they'd end up turning Kimberly into an orphan. So they agreed that only one of them should journey to Cambodia. The question was who should go. The intense give and take went on night after night.

"Jim, I have to go get Brendan. It's a mother's thing to do."

"Jan, it's nuts for you to go halfway around the world alone. Who knows what kind of situations and problems you'd run into?"

"You don't think women can travel halfway around the world alone? Only a man can do that? You don't think I can handle problems?"

"C'mon Jan, you know better than that. I know you're capable, but there are so many unknowns. So many things could go wrong. You know damn well, women can get taken advantage of easier than men. I'd be back here worried sick about you."

"I could do it Jim."

"I know, I know. But what about the money? Are you going to feel safe walking around Cambodia carrying thousands of dollars in cash?

Don't you think some crooks over there know the adoption game? Know that adoptive parents travel to Cambodia carrying thousands in cash? Don't you think you'd make an easy target by yourself?"

"We've never heard of that happening."

"You think someone's going to publicize it? It'd be pretty naïve to think that, with all the poverty throughout Cambodia, no Americans have ever been robbed over there."

Reason prevailed over passion. They both agreed that, just as a mother is the first to embrace a birth child, it was a mother's place to be the first to embrace an adoptive baby…but it was too risky for Jan to venture alone to Cambodia. Jim would go. Jan would be the backup. The decision was final until the night of July 16th.

◆ ◆ ◆

Jan and Jim had developed complete faith in the knowledge and experience of the West Coast International staff. If WCIAA said, as they did on the 14^{th,} that the adoption was a go, it must be so despite the chaos and uncertainty of recent weeks. With Jim's departure for Southeast Asia now only two weeks away, Jan and Jim decided it was time to tell Kimberly it was a done deal. After so many disappointments in the domestic adoption process, they had deliberately kept Kimberly out of the loop in the Saveth adoption saga, opting this time to wait for some degree of certainty rather than feed her more false hopes.

With eyes and ears like radar antennae, Kimberly had sensed something developing during the first half of July. She'd begun to say time and time again, "We're never gonna adopt, are we? I just know."

"Why do you say that?" Jan would ask.

"Because nothin's happened. We don't get any more of those phone calls from Shannon. I just know we're never going to."

So on a warm and beautiful Sunday afternoon, July 16th, Jan and Jim called Kimberly over to their small gazebo. "Kimberly, come over here, please. We want to tell you something."

"Ok. I'm coming," Kimberly replied as she readied her skates for promised roller-blading with Jim.

"Take a look at this picture," Jim said.

"Who's this?" Kimberly asked coyly.

"This is going to be your new baby brother. His name is Saveth right now, but it's going to be Brendan, and Saveth will be his middle name."

"He's so cute," Kimberly purred with a smile bright enough to light the darkest night.

After much more chatter about the new baby brother to be, and with Kimberly excited that he was to have the same first name as one of her neighborhood friends, she and Jim laced up and went off roller-blading in their large driveway. Jan went back inside relieved that Kimberly enthusiastically accepted the name Brendan. Jan had fully expected the independent-minded Kimberly to reject the proposed name in favor of one of her own.

Jan's jubilant moment in time was short-lived when, a few minutes later, she heard Jim yell for her from outside. She ran out to the driveway to find Jim bent over in pain. He told her he'd fallen. Jan could barely hide her concern. Jim was never the complaining type and was generally quite pain-tolerant.

"Jan, this isn't good. I'm hurt. This isn't good at all."

"What happened?"

"I fell…I've dislocated my shoulder."

Jan was temporarily speechless. Week after week of constant tension with the adoption process had frayed the nerves badly. She was overwhelmed with frustration and exasperation. When she found her voice, she simply declared, "You're not going, I'm going."

Jim looked at her and said, "No you're not. I'm going."

"No you're not, I'm going," Jan said again.

"I'm going," he said emphatically.

Jan, waking up to the absurdity of the argument finally said they had to get Jim to the Emergency Room. She pulled Jim's roller blades off and ran inside to get her car keys. After calling a neighbor to arrange for Kimberly's care, Jan ran back outside and was surprised to find Jim on the porch.

"It popped back in," he told Jan, still not quite believing it himself.

"Popped back in? How?"

"I was trying to get my shoes on, and without thinking, I bent over to tie my laces. When my arm swung down and around, the shoulder popped back in."

"Are you sure it's in?"

"Uh huh, it's in. I'm OK," Jim said, amazed with the whole episode, but still in obvious pain.

"Well, we're still going to the ER to get it checked out."

"Yeh, I think we'd probably better do that," Jim agreed.

They quickly put an ice pack on the shoulder and left for the Emergency Room, knowing that the usual ER triage system could have them waiting all night to see a doctor. And wait patiently they did as others with more urgent and life-threatening injuries and illnesses paraded through. Hours later, after x-rays, they found themselves talking with a young intern.

"Well," the doctor said, "it looks OK. The x-rays don't show any damage."

"Doctor, there's something you need to know. Jim's due to go to Cambodia in two weeks to bring back an adopted child. Do you think he should go?" Jan blurted. Ignoring Jim's glaring eyes, she went on to explain that Jim would be hauling a couple backpacks, a large Pullman travel bag, and an infant car seat, not to mention a baby as well on the return.

"Oh, well now," the young doctor began to worry. "I don't know about all that," and ran off to consult another doctor. When he returned, he said, "You really shouldn't go."

Jim was now starting to get angry at the whole situation. The doctor was saying just what Jan wanted to hear. She was the back-up quarterback just itching to get called into the game. She was ready. She knew the playbook to perfection...and she had received all the necessary vaccinations, just in case. All she needed was the nod from the coach.

"I'm going," Jim declared forcefully.

"No you're not. You can't take the chance. You can't go," Jan replied, feeling more confident with the doctor on her side.

"I'm going."

"No you're not. I'm going."

"I'm going and that's final," Jim said.

It was the driveway scene all over again until the doctor stepped in.

"Look," he said, "I'm ninety-eight percent sure you can make it over there and back. But what if it pops out again? What if complications develop and you need medical help? I personally would not want to be treated in a Cambodian hospital."

The issue was not going to be settled that night by a young resident doctor behind a curtain in an Emergency Room. The "I'm going" battlefront raged most of the way home from the hospital and then shifted all the way to the West Coast the next day when Jan consulted with West Coast International. After a brief description of the situation, the battle surge tilted in Jim's favor. WCIAA said the situation wasn't a problem. Dr. Hendrie from MAPS would be in Cambodia during the group adoption period. In fact, she'd be staying in the same hotel as Jim in Phnom Penh. Should Jim require medical assistance, no problem. With that assurance, Jan conceded the battle. Jim would be the one to go.

◆ ◆ ◆

Naively, Jan and Jim had planned to escape to New Hampshire's White Mountains for a few days of relaxation at the end of July in the week prior to Jim's departure to Cambodia. Final preparations for

Jim's journey went from high-gear hectic to overdrive frantic, making the idea of a restive getaway seem like something of a cruel joke. They cancelled their reservations.

While Jan concentrated on researching and booking final travel arrangements, Jim found himself on a frustrating scavenger hunt for the "right" cash. They had been told that Jim would need "crisp" new, uncirculated bills. He needed $6,000 in brand new $100's, $50's, $20's, and $10's. The bills had to be new, no folds, no creases, no wrinkles, no ATM marks. He also needed a hundred one dollar bills for tipping and small purchases. Jim called his bank and explained the situation and was told they could accommodate him. He went down to the bank on Monday and sat with the Head Teller to look over the cash. It was mostly used cash in good condition. He explained again what he needed the money for and how it had to be new, uncirculated cash. Once again, she said they could accommodate him on Wednesday when they would receive a shipment of new currency.

On Wednesday, Jim optimistically picked up the money and brought it home thinking he was all set. Jan sat down and went through the money, bill by bill, and discovered much of the money was not acceptable. Although the cash met the "crisp and new" criteria, it contained many unacceptable series dates. Supposedly, because of either money-laundering or counterfeit issues, Jan and Jim had been informed that bills dated between 1990 and 1996 would be rejected in Cambodia.

Jim went back to the bank where he and the sympathetic and understanding teller went to work on exchanging cash. After she went around to every teller station and obtained their new bills, she and Jim began the tedious process of review and selection or rejection of every bill. The process was extremely time-consuming and beyond the patience of the bank manager. Customer service in the bank was being compromised for a labor-intensive effort that would yield no profit to the bank. Jim left the bank with some but not all the money he needed.

By Friday, Jim was in a full court press, rushing from bank to bank in search of the needed cash.

"Do you have an account here, sir?"

"Uh, no, but you see, I…"

"Can't do it. You don't have an account here."

"But I…"

"Sorry."

Eventually, Jim ended up at his credit union to cash his paycheck. Jim had assumed that a small credit union would be unlikely to have the kind of new cash he needed. Surprise. Jim left with almost all the cash he needed. Jim was elated with his success, but as he made his way home, he felt himself getting more and more apprehensive. He didn't feel ready. The weekend was charging towards him like an enraged bull and he was standing there with a red cape in one hand and a bull-fighting manual in the other. What the hell ever made him think that a Cambodian adoption was a good idea?

11

Saturday, July 29, 2000

o o o o o o o o o o o o o o o o o o o o o o o o o o o o o o

My name is Saveth…but soon it will be Brendan Saveth. I am being given good care here at the orphanage. My caregivers wish me to be healthy and happy for the arrival of my new father in a few days. Buddha smiles upon me.

Jim lay quietly in bed. Although dog-tired from a hectic week, he'd tossed around in a restless sleep all night. His mind had refused to shut down, insisting instead on racing around from thought to thought in a manic review of all the week's activity, and worries of upcoming events. Jim felt like a silver ball inside a pinball machine, getting bounced madly from obstacle to obstacle, never stopping, never resting.

The week had been productive with he and Jan accomplishing the vast majority of preparatory tasks for his journey. Along the way, there had even been a moment or two of light-hearted humor, such as on Wednesday, when he ran around to several copying machines at his workplace, making final sets of documentation for everything. He wanted to have an extra set to take with him, and another for Jan to have at home. If everything went awry on the trip and his baggage got lost, Jan could fax or overnight express everything to him. Jan planned to get the extra copies notarized on Thursday.

Various colleagues questioned what he was doing with all the copying. A few knew about some of the previous attempts to adopt, but except for his boss, Jim had not told them about his plan to go to Cam-

Saturday, July 29, 2000   63

bodia. Whenever Jim told someone what he was doing, he felt he'd get a strange look. It was not a look of derision, but more of disbelief mixed with an inability to understand why anyone in his or her right mind would want to do such a thing. Jim would then pull out his wallet and show a picture of Saveth. Heads would nod and mouths would mumble something along the lines of, "Jeeze. Good luck."

One of Jim's friends at work, a former Marine Vietnam veteran who was a year younger than Jim, didn't hold back his personal view. "You're gonna do what? You hot ticket," he said, "you got guts. You got real guts. You're gonna go adopt a baby at your age? I'm on my third grandchild and you're going to Cambodia to adopt a baby? You hot ticket." Though Jim laughed loud and proudly during that Wednesday morning encounter, the full impact of what he was about to do finally hit him by nighttime.

So now, early Saturday morning, Jim was still pondering the "You're gonna do what?" reaction. The seriousness and enormity of the decision to travel to Cambodia had been more of a fantasy than a reality until Wednesday night. That's when it first hit him that he was not going on a vacation. It was not a frivolous adventure. It was not a TV game show prize. He was really going to journey into the heart of Southeast Asia with thousands of dollars strapped to his leg and waist in the hope of returning with an orphan baby. And assuming he was successful, he was then going to spend his male menopause years raising a child from a unique foreign culture. The incredulous "you're gonna do what?" statement echoed in his mind, but it was his own voice that he kept hearing. *Do I really know what I'm doing? Does it really make sense? What if I get out there and find out they won't release Brendan to me, or worse, they give him to me but then I can't get clearance to bring him back? What if...what if...what if? God, I'm gonna do what?*

For the prior two days, Jim had begun to fret about everything: the paperwork, the money, travel clothes, diseases, and foreign governments...not to mention foreign airlines. Although he and Jan enjoyed a trusting, sharing relationship, he avoided discussing his concerns with her. He wasn't sure why. Perhaps it was an ego or macho thing and he didn't want her to know that he was unsure of himself and the undertaking. Or perhaps he didn't want her worrying any more than she already was. Then he became frustrated with his festering second-guessing about everything. Surely, he thought, it was a normal reaction to all the information overload, all the warnings and advisories about travel to Southeast Asia, all the uncertainties about the impending moratorium on adoptions from Cambodia, all the comments by nay sayers about the difficulties of becoming an adoptive parent at mid-life. Of course he knew what he was doing. Of course he could do it. Of course he would do it. *Then what the hell am I worrying about. Get the hell out of bed and do something constructive. You're leaving for Cambodia tomorrow!*

As Jim began his busy day of final preparations, try as he might to keep a positive mindset, he couldn't shake a generalized feeling of foreboding. He realized it was somewhat irrational. *After all, I'm just going to Cambodia to adopt a baby just like thousands of other parents have done. It's not like I'm going to conquer Mt. Everest or heading off to war. Then again, some people get killed just going to the store to buy milk.*

Jim sat down and wrote a long rambling letter to Jan. In it he told her how much he loved her and Kimberly and how much happiness they brought to his life. He also told Jan where all the various insurance and financial records were located. He addressed the envelope to Jan with the notation, "In case I don't make it back from Cambodia" and placed it in his bureau. He forgot all about it and happened to come across it about a year later. When he showed it to her, Jan was floored with emotion. She was touched by his expression of love but shocked at how well his bravado at the time of the journey had masked his deep uncertainty and anxiety.

◆   ◆   ◆

Pack, pack, pack. Jim spent most of Saturday packing for the trip. It was his anti-anxiety therapy. It was necessary. It was constructive. It was mentally engaging because he had so much to pack, mindful of his own physical limitations and airline baggage limits. Since he'd received the airline tickets by FedEx only on Friday, he hadn't given much thought to airline baggage restrictions until then. When he saw the weight and size dimensions, he called China Air for clarification, thinking his luggage might exceed limitations. A discussion with the China Air representative resolved the confusion but still left him with the challenge of packing everything he needed in a manageable way. He had to think about not only what he could handle going over, but what he could handle in addition to carrying Brendan on the return.

He packed and repacked, checking and double-checking: medications, baby food, baby bottles, disposable diapers, baby clothing, his own toiletries, his own throw-away clothing, the car seat/baby chair, adoption documents, money, two money belts, passport and visa, critical phone numbers. The list seemed endless and continued to grow all day. The more he packed, the more he thought about other items he thought he should pack, such as clothes and toiletry items he and Jan wanted to donate to the orphanage and caregivers. Despite his daylong effort on Saturday, he would not snap the final snap and buckle the final buckle until mid-day Sunday, just hours before leaving.

Jim's packing activity on Saturday was interrupted a number of times. One of the major distractions came when Jan received a phone call from one of her work associates who was just that day returning with her husband from their journey to Cambodia. Despite many hurdles along the way, they returned successfully with their adopted child. However, she was calling to alert Jan and Jim that their return trip on China Air had been problematic. Despite having paid $600 for a seat for the baby, they boarded a full plane and were denied the seat. All manner of protest failed. She was calling Jan and Jim to warn them of the issue.

Jim immediately called China Air. The issue was more than simply getting something he had paid for. The issue was that he'd be airborne for some twenty-eight hours. He wouldn't have Jan or anyone else to take turns holding the baby. He'd most likely need to try to get a couple hours sleep. How could he do that or rest comfortably in the confines of an airline seat while holding the baby? He'd purchased a seat for Brendan to solve all the problems of trying to hold him in his lap for twenty-eight hours of flight time.

The agent at China Air was courteous and friendly. She assured Jim that he had nothing to worry about. The return seat for Brendan was booked. When Jim told her about the reason for his concern, she was extremely apologetic. She said she couldn't fathom a reason how something like that could have happened to his friends and promised to look into the situation. To help mitigate Jim's concerns, she provided him with the seat numbers for both himself and Brendan, and assured him once again that their reserved seats would not be given to any other passenger. Jim returned to his packing project.

◆ ◆ ◆

By early evening, the warm afternoon sun had retreated behind thick layers of darkening clouds. Jan looked apprehensively at the sky just before dark. The clouds looked ominous and threatening. She felt uncomfortable and checked the weather forecast. It wasn't good. A mid-summer storm was brewing to the south, along the Atlantic coast, and was poised to blow into southern New England by Sunday evening. Jan kept her concern about the weather to herself…Jim already had enough on his mind.

Both of them were destined to toss and turn for yet another night.

12

Sunday July 30, 2000

○ ○

My name is Kimberly, and today is a really exciting day. My Daddy is going to Cambodia to get my baby brother. I can't wait to hold him and help Mommy feed him. I told all my friends I'm getting a baby brother.

"Peace be with you," the man next to Jim said as he extended his arm for a handshake.

"Peace be with you," Jim mumbled in reply as he shook hands. His body was in church but his mind was in a million other places this morning. Cloudy skies caused the stained glass windows to appear dull and lifeless. The dim lighting in the church could not substitute for the missing splashes of sunlight, so the usually warm, womb-like atmosphere of the church seemed dreary and desolate. Jim prayed for a safe journey, but felt no comfort from his attendance at Sunday church service.

The rest of the morning flew by in a blur, and by noon, Jim was finally packed and ready to go. But instead of feeling confident and eager, he felt anxious and tense. While Jan and Kimberly went out for some last minute errands, Jim went for a brisk five-mile walk in an attempt to kill time and relieve his tension. Although there was some calming effect from the exercise and views of bucolic pastures along the backcountry roads, heavy overcast skies reinforced a gloomy feel to the day. Returning home before Jan and Kimberly, Jim jumped in his car and drove to town. Although the family had celebrated Kimberly's birthday in advance, and even though she would have another party with her neighborhood friends while Jim was away, he wanted to send her a surprise birthday card. He chose a cute card that he knew would elicit a happy giggle. Inside, he wrote a short note to Kimberly telling her how much he loved her and that he'd soon be "bringing home your baby brother".

Around five o'clock, Jan called the Providence airport to check on Jim's flight. She was told it was scheduled to leave on time at 8:55 pm. All was well, but Jan was still concerned about the approaching summer storm and simply could not shake an uneasy feeling that haunted her all day.

A quiet, candlelight dinner in some romantic out-of-the-way hideaway might have been what Jan and Jim needed this Sunday night, but that was not an option. The "last supper" family dinner was pleasant but less than relaxing. Jan and Jim were both up tight and couldn't stop themselves from needless review and nervous discussion of last-minute details about the trip. And Kimberly, of course, couldn't help herself from excited chattering about anything and everything.

Finally it was time. "OK, let's get going," Jim said, trying to sound confident and ready. "I've got to go get this done. Let's go."

As they drove to Providence Airport, they were grateful for the sparse Sunday evening traffic, but not for the darkening sky and the light rain which began to spatter against the windshield. The ride was quick and uneventful, and though it took only about three-quarters of an hour, it was still long enough for the usual "are we there yet?" queries from an impatient Kimberly.

Providence Airport is really T. F. Green Airport, and it is actually in Warwick, Rhode Island, not Providence. But as T. F. Green became bigger and busier in the 1990's as a spillover regional airport for travelers trying to avoid the numerous inconveniences of Boston's Logan Airport, it became customarily known and marketed as Providence Airport. After all, who had ever heard of Warwick other than local "Rhodies"? T. F. Green grew in popularity primarily because of its hassle-free access and relative efficiency as compared to the tribulations of getting in and out of Logan. Jan and Jim breezed right in to the airport, parked the car easily, and made their way to an nearly deserted American Airlines counter. But the joy of easy airport access was quickly replaced with a knot in the stomach when they saw a bulletin board stating that all flights were delayed because of thunderstorms across the Northeast. Jim's connecting flight on China Air was due to depart New York's JFK Airport at 11:55 pm. It was crucial that he make that flight to be able to get to Cambodia in time to pick up Brendan before the moratorium door slammed shut on Thursday.

The agent at the American Airlines check-in counter tried to be reassuring. He told Jan and Jim that there were some delays, but it was no big deal. When they went down to the loading gate, the American Airlines attendant there was giving the same pitch. He explained that although it was barely raining in Providence, there were severe thunderstorms at JFK where Jim's plane was originating. With no other apparent options, Jan, Jim and Kimberly took seats in the waiting area with a dozen plus other passengers, all waiting hopefully for the same flight.

As the minutes ticked away, Jan and Jim's apprehension grew exponentially. They knew that that if Jim missed the 11:55 pm China Air flight, there was no other flight available with China Air for two days…too late to get Brendan out of Cambodia before the moratorium. The American Airline attendant kept assuring them that Jim's flight to JFK would eventually depart and that the thunderstorms in New York would be delaying all flights out of that city, including Jim's flight on China Air. Jim would still make the connection.

By 10:00 pm, Jan and Jim's anxiety about the flights would no longer allow them to sit idle. After securing a blanket for Kimberly to keep her warm from a poorly regulated air conditioning system that had turned the waiting area into a refrigerator, Jan and Jim went into action. Jim called the China Air telephone number to try to verify if the 11:55 pm flight from JFK was going to be delayed. He could not get through to speak to a human attendant. The automated voice response system told Jim that his China Air flight was still scheduled to leave on time.

While Jim and the other passengers besieged the American Airlines gate attendant, Jan went back to the main American Airlines counter to see what else could be done. She eventually found herself in the office of a female AA representative who was very empathetic and went out of her way to see what could be done to help Jan and Jim out of their quandary. Laboring intensely on her computer terminal, she found alternate flights to Cambodia that would begin with an 8:30 am American Airlines flight from JFK to London, followed by a British Air flight to Singapore and flights on other airlines to Taipei and Cambodia. Jan ran back to the gate to tell Jim. By now it was approaching 11:30 pm and Jim along with the other passengers had been informed that the Providence to New York flight had been canceled. No other flights were available until the morning. The AA gate agent was feverishly rebooking the unhappy and impatient passengers.

Feeling extremely stressed but refusing to feel helpless, Jan and Jim explored their options. Few existed. The first problem was that there were no flights from Providence to New York early enough in the morning to get Jim to JFK in time for the 8:30 am flight to London. They then explored the possibility of bus transportation only to learn that there were no buses running from Providence to New York during the night. The third problem was that Jan was beginning to feel emotionally and physically exhausted. If they drove to New York, she felt she would never be able to make the drive back without falling asleep at the wheel. Besides that, there was the issue of putting Kimberly through this middle-of-the-night ordeal. A taxi to New York…that was the only answer. Jan came up with the idea of trying to get American Airlines to pay for a taxi. By then, the beleaguered American Airlines attendant had re-ticketed all the other passengers on next day flights to New York. While the disgruntled passengers either bedded down for the night or returned to their homes, Jan and Jim approached the attendant and began pleading their case, with Jan leading the verbal barrage.

"No way, lady. Are you kidding? A taxi to New York? Can't be done."

"But you have to," Jan pleaded, eventually breaking down into tears. "Don't you understand? We'll lose the baby we've worked so hard to get. You've got to help us."

"Look, I'd like to help, but there's no way I can authorize something like that."

"Please," Jan pleaded through her tears. "After five o'clock Thursday, we won't be able to get our baby. Jim has to get to New York tonight to catch an early flight to London tomorrow morning." More tears.

The attendant made a quick phone call to someone and then said, "OK, you probably just got me fired," as he began pounding away on his computer's keyboard. After a few minutes, he told Jim that he was unable to cancel his existing flights. Because Lotus Travel had booked the itinerary through China Air, only China Air could alter or cancel the itinerary. He directed Jim to go immediately to the China Air counter upon arriving in New York to get the flights canceled before going to the American Airlines counter to book the new itinerary worked out by the helpful AA customer service agent that Jan had spoken with earlier. He handed Jan and Jim a written authorization for the taxi and directed them to an office in the main lobby area. After retrieving Jim's luggage, they rushed to the main lobby. Jan and Jim were unable to locate whoever it was that they were supposed to see about the taxi. They then sought out Jan's helpful customer service agent who directed them to a tiny hole-in-the-wall office where another female agent greeted them. She obviously had already been given a heads-up about the taxi deal and proceeded to call in one of the waiting taxi drivers to negotiate a fare to New York. After a bit of haggling over whether the price should be $450 or $475, a deal was struck with a driver named Bob. He reached for his cell phone, called his wife to tell her that he was taking a fare to New York, and with a quick "OK, let's go," led Jan, Kimberly and Jim through the lobby and outside to his cab parked near the passenger pick-up area. Bob was a tall, strapping man, over six feet tall, and Jan and Jim had to break into a half-run to keep up with him. Kimberly, who had been an uncomplaining little trooper through the whole ordeal, trotted alongside.

As they sprinted through driving rain to the parked taxi, Jan and Jim both wrestled with last second thoughts about the way things were going. For her part, Jan had envisioned a lovely late Sunday afternoon drive to Providence airport where she and Kimberly would lovingly send Jim off on his round-the-world baby quest flight. The parting would be emotional, for sure, but hopeful and mutually comforting. Jim, having silently and stoically battled his inner demons of doubt and trepidation for the past week, was similarly unhappy with this uncertain, hurried departure.

As Bob threw Jim's luggage into the trunk of the taxi, Jan and Jim stood in the pouring rain and looked into each other's eyes. Neither liked what they saw. Jan uncontrollably blurted out what she was thinking, "What are we doing?" She didn't even hear herself saying it. For a second or two, Jim felt like he was watching a movie. He saw himself and his family standing there in the eerie glow of the halogen streetlights, trying to ignore the sheets of pelting rain. A car drove slowly by, its windshield wipers dancing in a frenzy, but Jim saw them as if in slow motion. Everything seemed momentarily unreal. Jim snapped himself out of the trance and knelt down to face Kimberly, ignoring the wet sidewalk. She looked at him, sensed his apprehension, and said, "Daddy, what are you going to do?" Jim looked at her as courageously as he could and replied, "I'm going to go get your little baby brother."

As Kimberly bear-hugged Jim, he felt a surge of newfound energy. It was as if Kimberly had magically bestowed supernatural powers to him that would enable him to accomplish his mission. He quickly gave Kimberly a kiss on the cheek, and stood up as soldierly as he could to hug Jan. Fighting back tears, he mumbled, "I gotta go," as Jan and Kimberly broke down crying, knowing this really was goodbye. He jumped into the back seat of the taxi, and the driver helpfully gunned the taxi away immediately. As the car sped away from the curb, Jim couldn't stop himself from looking back at his tearful wife and daughter. It was a mistake. Through the shimmering streetlight and rain-spattered taxi window, Jan could clearly see Jim's face and saw in it a frightening reflection of fear and desperation that she had never seen before. *"What the hell are we doing?"* she asked herself in bewilderment before once again breaking down in tears that matched the pouring rain.

Kimberly, with childlike faith that all would be well, became the anchor in this emotional storm. She grabbed Jan, pulled her tight, and reached up as she said, "Mommy, Daddy told me to give you a kiss from him for every single day that he's gone, so I'm going to start early." With that she gave Jan a warm kiss on the cheek. Jan scooped her up and ran through the rain to their car, crying even more. As they ran in the dark and the rain, Kimberly kept repeating, "Don't worry, Mommy. Daddy's gonna be home in a week. Don't worry."

13

Middle of the Night
Monday AM, July 31, 2000

○ ○

My name is Kimberly, and it's way, way past my bedtime so I'm sleeping on the back seat of Mommy's car. We brought Daddy to the airport a long time ago, but everything got messed up because of the rain. It was really, really boring at the airport, but I was good because I want a baby brother.

With post-midnight traffic virtually non-existent, the task should have been simple: drive home; go to bed. But Jan should have known, nothing was going to be easy this night. As she accelerated north on Interstate 95, the rain started coming down in torrents, hammering the windshield in windblown waves, making visibility extremely poor and making a dark night even darker. Forced to slow down to drive very cautiously, she nevertheless drove straight past the sign for her turn-off onto Route 146. She was too distracted, reliving the past several hours and imagining what lay ahead for Jim. She snapped out of her stupor when she saw the signs for Route 495 and suddenly realized that she had traveled miles beyond her Route 146 exit.

Jan pulled into the first lighted service station she saw to get directions. It was a self-serve all-night station with a small booth for an attendant. Not wanting to wake Kimberly by opening and closing the car door, Jan drove around the gas pump islands and pulled up alongside the cashier booth. She could see the immediate look of suspicion and fear on the young attendant's face as she opened her window to speak to him. She quickly explained that she had a sleeping child in the back seat and needed directions. Relieved that the station wasn't being robbed, he did his best to give her directions for how to get back to Route 146 by cutting through Woonsocket, Rhode Island. She drove off optimistically, only to soon find herself lost in a run-down section of the old mill town. The darkness and rain made the dilapidated houses and boarded-up businesses look even more uninviting and downright threatening. Physically spent, emotionally drained and feeling extremely vulnerable, Jan asked herself again and again, "What are we doing? Just what are we doing?"

Having no choice but to persevere, she drove down one darkened avenue after another, trusting to instinct for direction, and praying she would eventually come across some road signs leading to Route 146. After what seemed like an eternity, she did find her highway. Driving as fast as the storm conditions would allow, she finally arrived home after 3:00 am. Kimberly never awoke as Jan carried her into the house, undressed her and tucked her into bed. Worrying about how Jim was doing, Jan crawled into bed and immediately fell into an exhausted sleep.

◆ ◆ ◆

Jim sat silently in the back seat as the taxi sped towards New York. Fortunately, he had no way of knowing about Jan's difficulties in getting home from Providence Airport as he wondered to himself: how the hell am I ever going to pull this off?

There had been no communication between him and Bob, the taxi driver, since leaving the airport except for a brief commentary by Bob as they left. "So you're going to adopt a child. That's a wonderful thing you're going to do, a wonderful thing." Jim had thanked him for the thought and they had both fallen silent.

After a while, Jim got tired of speculating how things would go once he got to JFK and attempted to initiate some conversation with Bob by asking, "I suppose you do this often?" Jim assumed that any taxi driver working Providence Airport would end up making occasional runs to New York and JFK, especially for harried businessmen and businesswomen with urgent appointments or connections in New York. An already beleaguered Jim was not happy to hear Bob say, "Nope, first time." And he felt no surge of assurance when the taxi driver quickly added, "but I've been to New York before."

"How long do you think it'll take to get there?" Jim asked, trying to figure out how much time he'd have to cancel the China Air flights and try to book the new itinerary the American Airline agent had worked up. He was also thinking it might be nice to catch a couple hours of sleep in the JFK terminal before boarding the flight to London.

"Don't really know," Bob replied, "depends on the traffic."

Jim looked out the window at the solitary cars that could be seen from time to time on the rain-soaked interstate highway. What traffic? Jim guessed that they might make it to JFK by 3:00 am, for sure before 4:00. That should give him plenty of time to get everything squared away long before the 8:30 am American Airline flight to London.

Probably sensing Jim's tension, Bob began a rambling chitchat about his personal experience with the Far East. He told Jim that he met his wife in Korea and lived there for several years before returning to the states. His Korean wife already had children when he met her and he did not father any additional children with her. Of greater interest to Jim was the taxi driver's recounting of trips he and his wife had taken back to Korea. The downside, he told Jim, was the length of the flight. It seemed to go on forever, especially if a traveler was unable to sleep through at least a few hours of it. The upside of flying to the Far East was the superiority of the major Asian airlines to U.S. carriers. The taxi driver said they offered better service and even provided gifts to passengers. He also told Jim that Hong Kong had one of the most beautiful airports in the world and Jim would enjoy his short stopover there to catch his connecting flight to Cambodia.

After a while, they ran out of conversation and Jim dozed off for a short time, but the rain beating violently against the windshield and roof of the taxi soon awakened him. From Jim's view in the back seat, it seemed impossible that Bob could see where he was going. The rain fell in a frightening torrent. Even at fast speed, the windshield wipers were useless. It was like driving through a waterfall. Jim leaned forward, immediately wide-awake.

"Can you see OK?" asked Jim, not able to see beyond the hood of the car.

"I just straddle the lane lines," Bob replied, a technique made possible by the absence of traffic.

Jim leaned back and tried to relax as Bob navigated along the deserted stretch of Interstate 95. There was enough weighing on his mind without concerning himself about Bob's driving ability. He stared out his window into the darkness and tried to think of nothing. After a while, as they approached more populated areas of southwest Connecticut and crossed over into New York, the rain lessened and visibility became much better. The black curtain over isolated areas of Route 95 gave way to bright splashes of sodium light that illuminated alternating areas of industrial development and residential neighborhoods that had been built alongside the highway. Thinking of his peaceful two acres tucked away in the central Massachusetts countryside, Jim wondered how people could tolerate the constant noise and fumes of heavy Interstate traffic in their backyards. Kids must play inside all the time, he thought. What a way to live!

As Bob began making his way through the Bronx section of New York City, he asked Jim if he could spot any signs for JFK Airport. At one point, passing through a construction area, Bob made a wrong turn and soon found himself headed down a dead end gravel roadway leading to the East River. He was able to back up, get on the proper highway, and then onto the Whitestone Bridge, which took them across the river from the Bronx into Queens. As they passed Flushing, New York, a brightly lit, empty Shea Stadium appeared like a ghostly apparition. Jim wondered why the stadium was all lit up like that in the middle of the night. It certainly looked quiet and peaceful at three o'clock in the morning, quite in contrast to it's reputation as the noisiest outdoor ballpark in the majors…not because of 55,000 boisterous New York fans, but due to its location in the direct flight path to La Guardia Airport.

Jim sighed a silent relief as brightly lit signs soon heralded the entrance to JFK. As the taxi driver circled around the many access roads trying to locate the China Air terminal, Jim looked out the window and marveled at how quiet and deserted a major airport could be in the middle of the night. His mission almost over, Bob drove like a man possessed, looking desperately for the terminal, eventually driving into a huge, partially enclosed, garage-like terminal area. Suddenly, Jim heard Bob exclaim, "OK, there it is. There's China Air." Wasting no time after pulling up in front of a sign for China Airlines, Bob jumped out of the cab, quickly pulled Jim's luggage out of the trunk, and then stood there expectantly. Jim looked at him and wondered if the taxi driver was waiting for a tip. From the negotiations that went on at Providence Airport, he knew Bob was going to receive half of the $475 fare, which meant that the taxi driver was averaging close to $40 per hour for the round trip to New York. After an awkward moment or two, Jim, feeling stupid, asked, "Do I tip you?"

"That would be nice," Bob answered.

Jim was clueless as to whether or not he should be tipping and wondered if the negotiated fare by American Airlines included a tip. What's the difference? Jim had much more important things to get to. He handed Bob a $20 bill and turned to look at his luggage bags to be sure he had everything. The taxi driver took the twenty, jumped back into his cab, and drove off in the blink of an eye. By the time Jim turned around to say goodbye, Bob was speeding off. Jim shrugged it off and looked around. Everything appeared closed. There was no sign of life at China Air or at any of the adjacent terminals. Jim took a deep breath, grabbed his bags, and walked to the glass doors under the China Airlines sign.

The electronic sensors controlling the entrance doors "saw" Jim approaching and the doors slid open for him as majestically as the waters had parted for Moses. Jim walked hesitantly into the China Air terminal, finding it eerily empty. A floor to ceiling glass wall blocked entry to the terminal service area. The only sign of life was a cleaning crew working on the other side of the metal detector gateways. Seeing no other option, Jim decided to go over to talk to the cleaners. As he approached the rope stanchions near the metal detectors, a head bobbed up and looked at Jim. The man was seated behind the metal detector and did nothing but look quizzically at Jim until Jim called him over, asking to speak with him.

The man was surprisingly young looking to Jim. He was dressed neatly with a blazer and slacks. On his jacket lapel was an ID security badge.

"I missed my flight with China Air. I need to go down to the China Air counter to rebook my flights," Jim told the young security guard.

"You can't go down there. We're closed."

"You're closed? What do you mean you're closed?" Jim asked.

The young security guard spoke in circles, leaving Jim confused. He wore a constant smile and spoke pleasantly, but made no sense. Jim thought the guard acted as if he was on drugs, or as if he was learning disabled.

"You don't understand," Jim persisted. "I've got to talk with someone from China Air. Can I go down there and wait for them to open?" The huge glassed-in area they were standing in was completely empty, without chairs or benches. An overactive air conditioner, like the one in Providence, made the place ice-cold.

As Jim unsuccessfully continued to try to communicate with the young man, another security guard, a female, appeared on the scene. Jim now spoke to her.

"I've got to get in to see the people at China Airlines. How do I do that? Can't I just go down to their counter area and sit and wait for them to reopen? I need to rebook a flight to Cambodia that I missed earlier tonight."

"China Air doesn't open until five o'clock," she replied calmly.

"Really? Well, that's why I need to go down there…so I can talk to them as soon as they open."

"You don't understand, they don't open until 5:00 pm."

"Five pm? Five pm? What do you mean 5:00 pm?"

"All their flights go out at night so that travelers arrive over there in the daytime. They're on the other side of the world. There's no point in them leaving here during the day and arriving in the middle of the night."

"Oh no," Jim cried in shocked realization. "You've got to be kidding! Well, I've got to do something now. What can I do? Where can I go? What airlines are open now?"

"There's nothing open in this terminal, and you can't stay here anyway. We're closed for an overnight security sweep. A security crew with dogs will be going over every inch of this place. You have to leave," she said as she left to answer an unseen phone ringing nearby.

"Where can I find American Airlines?" Jim asked the young guard who remained standing there with his fixed smile. Thankfully, the man made enough sense for Jim to understand that American was located in another terminal some distance away. He'd have to take a shuttle bus to get there, a blue shuttle bus.

Jim went outside to wait for the bus. A woman was sitting on a bench by herself. She hadn't been there earlier when Jim arrived by taxi and he wondered where she came from. She started talking to Jim as soon as he put down his luggage. It was obvious that she was angry and upset, and wanted to vent to anyone within hearing distance. She claimed she had spent two and a half hours sitting in a plane on a JFK runway before her flight was cancelled. The plane returned to the terminal and all passengers had to disembark and reschedule other flights for the morning.

Jim felt a twinge of hope. Some flights at JFK had obviously been cancelled. Maybe, despite the automated phone attendant message to the contrary, just maybe his China Air flight had really been cancelled after all. But after thinking about that remote possibility for a minute or two, he decided his best course of action was to find American Airlines and try to book the new itinerary that the helpful agent in Providence had outlined.

Jim waited and waited for a bus to come by. The lady on the bench called someone on her cell phone and talked on and on about having spent two and a half hours sitting on the runway only to be taken back to the terminal and be put off the plane. She groused about how the airlines didn't really care about people and how they mistreated people. While she ranted and raved, Jim spotted a bus passing by on a lower road. When she got off the phone, Jim talked to her about the shuttle buses since she had given the impression that she traveled often from JFK. She confirmed what he now suspected: the shuttle buses did not come up to where he was waiting. He would need to walk down to the lower access road. Jim wished her well, picked up his bags, and began trudging down the long ramp towards the lower road.

Finding an abandoned luggage cart near the end of the sidewalk, Jim felt a little bit lucky for the first time since leaving home. His good luck continued as he pushed the cart along the road and a blue shuttle bus approached. Jim flagged the bus down and told the bus driver he wanted to go to the American Airlines terminal. The driver, a foreign national who spoke very little English, tried to tell Jim that he needed the red shuttle bus. Desperate to get somewhere closer to American Airlines, Jim explained that a security guard told him very explicitly that he needed the blue shuttle bus. Remembering the young security guard's blank stare and fixed smile, Jim quickly assumed the foreign bus driver must know what terminals he drove to, but he felt this bus must be able to take him closer to American Airlines than where he was now. Hearing the distress in Jim's voice, the bus driver told Jim, "Okay, okay. I take you to end of line. You get off. Wait for red bus." Jim threw his bags on the bus, relieved to be going someplace, anyplace.

When the bus driver reached the end of his loop, he told Jim this was where he had to get off and wait for the red bus. Jim alighted from the bus to find several men and women standing around. *This is good,* Jim thought, *at least I've got some other people to hang around and wait with.* Jim quickly noticed that they didn't have any luggage, just cameras and video equipment. Catching snatches of animated conversation, Jim deduced that they were waiting for some important dignitary to arrive. Shortly, a car pulled up and the driver excitedly told them that the person they were waiting for was coming in at some other part of the airport. They all piled into the car and took off in pursuit of their news story, leaving Jim once again standing alone in front of a deserted JFK international terminal.

A lone taxicab slowly circled the terminal. Jim was momentarily tempted to flag the cab but suppressed the urge. Not knowing how far he was from the American Airlines terminal, he thought it silly to be taking a cab from one part of the airport to another. *Hell with it. The shuttle bus has got to be coming by soon.* But the shuttle bus didn't come by anytime soon and Jim regretted not flagging the taxi. The only other opportunity he had for a ride was from a man cruising the area who drove up next to Jim, smiled, and propositioned Jim in a sweet, suggestive voice, "Would you like a ride?" Jim spat out an emphatic "No".

One by one, the minutes dragged by. It was an agonizingly slow parade of time and Jim was beginning to lose patience and confidence. It was now past four o'clock in the morning and the first hint of daylight began to slightly brighten the night sky. Jim was wrestling with a growing fatigue that he couldn't ignore or wish away. He was getting the "blahs" and feeling a crunch on his energy level. *Jeez. I've got to pull together here. Can't think about sleep. I don't know how, but I've got to pull together here. I've gotta rally.*

An old, heavy-set black man ambled out of the terminal. He had the look of a night janitor. He stood near the door and lit a cigarette. Happy to see any sign of life at this point, Jim walked over to talk with him.

"Say, do you know where the American Airlines terminal is?"

"Ova dere. See dat terminal ova dere?" the old man replied through tight lips that hid a toothless mouth. He pointed to the outline of another large building in the distance. "Dat's da amerykin airline ova dere. Ova da uddah side ah da hyway."

"Really? Thanks. But how do you get there?" Jim asked hopefully.

"Gots to go over da road, and around, and up anuddah road."

"Okay. Great. I'll walk over there."

"No, no. C'aint do dat. C'aint do dat. Dat's a hyway. You drive dere. C'aint walk."

"But how do I do that? There's no shuttle bus coming by. No cabs. How do I get there?"

The old man shrugged, flipped his cigarette butt into the gutter, and returned inside. Jim watched him disappear and quickly determined he was going to walk over to the American Airlines terminal. He simply had to.

Jim picked up his bags and started down the long sidewalk, and once again, he found an abandoned luggage cart near the sidewalk's end. Buoyed by his good fortune and energized by a visible goal, he began pushing his cart down the empty road. Within a few minutes, he had made his way about a quarter of a mile along the road and was partway up the ramp to the bridge that passed over the highway below. Suddenly, seemingly from nowhere, a car's headlights shone brightly on him and his cart, as a New York police car pulled up alongside. The lone policeman in the cruiser rolled down his window.

"Where ya going? Ya not supposed t'be up here."

"I've got to get to American Airlines," Jim explained. "I couldn't connect with a cab or a shuttle bus. I have to get over there," he said, pointing to the building about a quarter mile away.

"Ya can't walk over there. Go back," the policeman ordered coldly, without any apparent concern for Jim's need to get to the terminal.

"Look, I've really got to get there. Can you give me a hand?"

"What's it say on the side on my car, Bub? New York Police. This ain't no cab. Get back," he ordered.

"Thanks a lot," Jim replied sarcastically, but then quickly turned his cart around to head back the way he came. He figured the last thing he needed at this point was a trip to the local lockup. The policeman watched Jim turn around before driving off, apparently satisfied that he had just made the world a better and safer place.

Jim once again took up his lone sentry position near the international terminal. He stood dejectedly in the steady cold mist feeling alone and alienated. He was tired and frustrated. He chided himself with the irony of it all…standing around with six thousand dollars strapped to his body, but unable to get to a building that stood only about a half mile away. *What do I do now? What can I do? Darn!*

As time went by, a couple buses rounded the corner and stopped a short distance from where he stood. Each time, Jim eagerly picked up and shouldered his bags in preparation to board, only to see a bright "Employees Only" sign at the front of the bus. One time he ran over to the bus to ask if he could hop a ride to the American Airlines terminal. No, he was told, he'd have to wait for the shuttle. When he replied that he'd been waiting forever for a shuttle that never came, he was told to just be patient, one would come. And eventually, one did.

It was around 5:00 am, when Jim finally dragged himself into the American Airlines terminal building. *Boy, am I doing great. I've been gone from home for almost a half day and I haven't flown a single mile towards Cambodia. Yikes, beyond a scheduled flight to London, I don't even have a way to get to Cambodia. What…in…the…world…am…I…doing?*

14

Early Morning
Monday, July 31, 2000

○ ○
My name is Saveth. Something is amiss. There is much talk and activity here at the orphanage. My nursemaid rocks me, hugs me, and whispers in my ear that all will be well. Buddha is with me.

Jim forgot about how sleepy and tired he was as soon as he entered the American Airlines terminal. When he stepped off the escalator on the terminal's main level, he immediately felt as if he had magically rejoined the human race. In contrast to his past few hours of lonely highways and deserted terminals, Jim walked into a bustling environment where hundreds of travelers teemed about or stood in line to check into outbound flights. The American Airlines ticket counter seemed to stretch forever and Jim could see dozens of ticket agents busily servicing customers. *Why the heck didn't I come here first,* Jim scolded himself...even before discovering that the JFK American Airlines terminal remained open twenty-fours hours a day.

He spotted a sign for a food court and decided he needed a quick coffee before getting in line at the ticket counter. He ordered a coffee and bagel with cheese. Not accustomed to New York prices, he discovered the small coffee was two dollars and the bagel was also two dollars. In a weak attempt at humor, Jim inquired, "How much without the cheese?" The bleary-eyed, minimum wage server smiled wryly, and shot back, "Two bucks."

Jim felt new life surge through his veins with the first swallow of warm coffee. He no longer felt alone against the world. No longer abandoned. Orphaned? But what world was it that he now found himself in? It wasn't the one he left. As he surveyed the large food court while he savored his bagel and coffee, he saw a rag-tag collection of people who all looked like foreigners to him. Any loud conversation that reached his ears was non-English. *Wow, they talk about New York being the melting pot of America. They're not kidding.* Then thinking about how tired and bedraggled he must look to others, he figured he probably blended right in with some street people he saw wandering around the food court. *Except I've got six thousand dollars strapped to my body.* And he was struck by all the New York Yankee hats. It seemed to him that half the people in the food court wore such a cap. He laughed to himself. He had a Yankee's cap stuffed in his duffle bag. He was tempted to dig it out and wear it, thinking he'd fit in better with New Yorkers and maybe get better service. But a glance at his watch told him he needed to get going.

As he shuffled towards the ticket counters with his bulky luggage, he passed a sign for a men's restroom. Great. He rushed in, only to gag immediately on the stomach-turning stench that filled the place. The place smelled so bad he instinctively held his breath. A quick look around the huge restroom revealed dirty sinks, overflowed toilets, and urinals that looked as if they hadn't been flushed for days. And the floor everywhere was wet and sticky to his feet. No way would he put his bags down on that floor. He immediately ran out of the restroom, deciding he could hold out until he boarded the plane.

Debating which line to get into, Jim spotted an American Airlines customer service "greeter" who walked among the hundreds of early morning travelers, providing answers to questions and giving directions to confused passengers who found themselves standing in the wrong lines. Jim approached the AA attendant and briefly explained his situation.

"Follow me. Let's see if we can get you some help," the attendant responded in a tone of voice that seemed to validate his words. He led Jim over to a cheery-faced, black female ticket agent who listened intently to Jim's tale of woe. She studied the proposed itinerary that had been worked out by the agent at T.F. Green and then began banging away on her computer keyboard, practiced fingers dancing deftly across the keys while her eyes remained fixed on screens that flashed across her computer monitor. She spoke aloud as she worked, sometimes speaking to Jim, sometimes speaking to herself.

"No good," she finally said.

"Huh?"

"No good. That British Air flight from London to Singapore is booked solid."

"They told me I could probably get on as a standby," Jim explained.

"No way. The flight is actually showing overbooked. Ain't no standby going to get on that flight. They'll be looking for people to take a bump. You'd be making a mistake trying to get standby on that flight"

Jim's early elation and optimism after being brought over to the agent instantly tanked, and he again became aware of how weary he was getting. She seemed to read his mind.

"Now, hold on, hold on. We gonna get you there. There's no quit in this old gal. Gimme a minute," she assured Jim as her eyes darted from screen to screen. She tossed out different scenarios and possibilities. None of them worked out right. Jim would either not beat the adoption moratorium deadline, or be scheduled to arrive so close under the wire that if there were any other delays along the way, all would be for naught.

"Well, this is your best bet," she finally declared. "This is a flight with Thai Airlines. It's a first class ticket, a Royal Executive Flight."

She paused for a moment before adding, "It'll cost you five thousand dollars."

She glanced past her computer monitor and saw Jim's face telegraph his sinking feeling. *Holy smokes! Five thousand dollars! You've got to be kidding!* Suddenly, Jim started to feel that the six thousand dollars in his money belts was more like petty cash than a small fortune.

"I can also put you on a flight outta JFK at noon today with a London connection on a flight that's going to have an eight-hour layover in Ho Chi Ming City. That one'll cost you four thousand."

Besides the long layover, that flight would get Jim to Cambodia late Wednesday with very little time to get through the bureaucratic maze needed to effect the adoption before the moratorium at five o'clock Thursday afternoon. *Boy, that's calling it close.*

Seeing Jim wrestle with his dilemma, she went out of her way to be empathetic and helpful.

"Look honey, you go think this over for a bit. You go think about this. Once you decide, you come right back here to see me. Don't go standing in any lines. You come see me. I'll work you in."

Jim thanked her profusely and went directly in search of a phone to call Jan.

◆ ◆ ◆

The shrill sound of the telephone jarred Jan from a deep sleep. Through eyes that reluctantly opened to peer at the alarm clock, she saw it was just after 7:00 am. *Jim! It must be Jim.* She grabbed at the bedside phone, adrenalin surging through her body like an electric charge. But the charge was carrying only negative current. She had gone to bed in the middle of the night assuming that Jim would be taking an early flight from JFK to London as the first leg of his revised itinerary. *He shouldn't be calling me at this time.*

"Jim?"

"Jan."

"Jim, what's happening? Where are you?"

"You wouldn't believe it. You couldn't imagine the night I've had," Jim said in a voice cracking with dejection and exhaustion.

Jan listened in dismay as Jim briefly recounted the details of his journey from Providence, the closed China Air terminal, the time standing out in the night rain, the failed attempt to reach the American Airlines terminal by foot, the callous rebuff by one of New York's Finest, and finally the shocking news that the only suitable flight would cost five thousand dollars…and it wasn't guaranteed. The ticketing could only be finalized with Thai Airlines when he reached Heathrow Airport. In his rapid-fire telling of the events, Jan heard eight thousand dollars, and with each word he uttered, she became more and more worried about her Jim. The pitiful sounding wretch on the other end of the line was not the vibrant, hard-charging Jim she had known and loved for years.

"Come home."

"What?"

"Come home, Jim. Either I'll come get you or take a flight home. Whatever. Just come home."

Jan's words hit Jim like a bucket of ice water. All of the years of thinking and talking about adoption, and the past two years of wasted effort and frustration in trying to adopt domestically flashed through his numbed mind. *Come home? Come home? How can I come home now? After all we've gone through? Come home without Brendan? I'm not coming home. No way. This is do or die. I've got to get this done.*

"No, Jan. I'm going through with this."

Jan heard the stubborn determination in Jim's voice. She was extremely concerned about him but could sense that it would be futile to try to dissuade him. She felt that if he got some rest, he'd be all right. But because of their tired minds and emotion-clouded thinking, their discussion of proposed flight itineraries resulted in several miscommunications. Jan mistakenly thought that Jim would have a first class seat from New York to London that would allow him to stretch out and get some much needed sleep. Jim either mistakenly said eight thousand instead of five thousand, or she heard eight instead of five.

"Okay, Jim, but if you're going to go, just get to London now and take the eight thousand dollar flight. Don't go to Ho Chi Ming City. I don't want you stranded there for eight hours, or god knows how long. Even if all went well with the four thousand dollar itinerary, you might not get there in time to get Brendan before the moratorium kicks in. Get on that eight-thirty London flight."

"But what about the five thousand dollars?"

"Don't worry about the money. I'll fight with American Airlines about the eight thousand dollars."

"Are you sure?"

"Yes, yes. Take the flight to London. I'll battle with American Airlines this week. It's their fault you missed the China Air flight. I'll fight with them about the increased costs."

"Okay, okay," Jim said, instantly fueled by the encouragement he heard through the phone. "But I gotta go now, I gotta go. It's almost seven-thirty. If I'm gonna make that eight-thirty flight, I gotta go right away."

"Good luck."

They reluctantly hung up the phones.

Jim spotted another abandoned cart near the phone bank. He threw his luggage on the cart and ran back to the helpful female ticket agent as fast as he could. As she had directed, he bypassed the lines and stood near her ticket window while she finished with another passenger.

As he stood waiting, bedlam broke out at the next agent over. A group of Hispanic passengers were jabbering loudly among themselves while one of the group yelled at the flustered ticket agent. Based on the group's composition, Jim quickly assumed that they were an extended family, from grandparents to grandchildren. It appeared they were homebound out of the country…and were trying to take everything they owned with them.

"Sir, you cannot take the air conditioner on the plane," the ticket agent repeated as politely as she could.

The family had mountains of battered suitcases and boxes, three coolers tied shut with clothesline rope, and an unboxed window air conditioner. There were several young men, some young women, several children and possibly a grandmother. In addition to the air conditioner issue, they were apparently missing some passports or other necessary documentation. To top it all off, they didn't have enough flight tickets for all of them. The besieged ticket agent called in a supervisor and a bilingual agent just as Jim's agent called him to her neighboring counter.

As Jim's agent worked on his tickets, the spectacle at the next counter went on and on.

"Why we can't take air conditioner?" screamed one of the young bilingual men.

"Because it contains Freon gas and it's not allowed on the plane," the supervisor explained.

"Freon? What we care about Freon. What is that, Freon?"

The children were yelling, chasing, and punching one another with the exception of one young boy who kept coming over to Jim's counter. He would simply look at Jim with a blank expression and then suddenly try to grab Jim's luggage cart and tow it away. Jim felt silly, engaging in a tug of war with the child, but he had no choice. Meanwhile, the circus at the next window continued as the police were finally called in when the belligerent young man began making verbal threats to the American Airline personnel. One of the other young men climbed atop one of the piles of their luggage and indicated that he was going to stage a sit down strike right there unless they were all allowed to board with all their belongings.

When Jim's ticket agent announced that he was all set, he was relieved to be leaving the chaos. Glancing at the clock on the wall he asked her if she thought he still had time to make the flight. She assured him he did and called over a roving customer service agent to help get Jim and his luggage to his flight since it was too late for the ticket agent to send the luggage to the plane by the conveyor belt system. As they dashed off towards the gate area, two large black female security guards suddenly stood in their way.

"Where you goin' boy? Where you goin'?"

"I'm going to catch my flight."

"Well, we gonna look in dem bags you got, boy."

"But these are going on the plane with me."

"We gonna check 'em first."

Jim glanced at his large bags. He had bound them tightly with bright yellow masking tape for identification and security. Jim looked at the American Airlines agent who shrugged helplessly.

"I'm going to miss my plane," Jim pleaded to no avail as he frantically tore at the tape and opened the locks.

To his great relief, they only spent a couple seconds rummaging through the open bags. Then they told him to go on to his flight. They would get the bags on his plane for him. Again the AA agent shrugged helplessly as he rushed off with Jim, and worse, he muttered to Jim, "They'll never get those bags on that plane." *Oh, please God, let them get my bags on the plane.* Jim comforted himself with the knowledge that he had all the most important items in his carry-ons, including all the documents needed for the adoption. *I've got six grand. If they lose my bags on me, I'll just buy what I need along the way.*

The American agent led Jim through the JFK maze towards his gate area. He finally pointed Jim around another turn and wished him well. Jim jogged around the corner to find long lines at the metal detectors leading to his gate. His heart skipped a beat. It was quarter past eight and he saw no way that he was going to get to his plane before it took off. Every time the line moved a little bit, the detector would beep and a passenger would be sent back to empty his or her pockets and try to go through again. Beep! Beep! Beep! Jim was fit to scream. He felt like a character in a Fellini movie. The world was simply a mad place, or at the very least, the human condition was excruciatingly maddening.

Then, as if in answer to his desperate, silent plea, security agents activated a third metal detector. Jim rushed to be first in line, being uncharacteristically impolite to man, woman, child…even old ladies…as he aggressively surged towards the new lane.

Jim threw his bag on the x-ray conveyor and held his breath as he walked briskly through the metal detector. No beep. *Oh, thank god.* He grabbed his bags off the end of the conveyor and ran towards his gate. He could see the attendant moving to close the door to the boarding ramp as he neared the gate.

"Hold it," Jim yelled to a startled attendant.

After checking Jim's boarding pass, he allowed Jim to enter the jetway to the plane. Jim ran down the ramp just as a male flight attendant prepared to close the door to the plane. Huffing and puffing with sweat pouring down his face, Jim showed his ticket to a young female attendant who greeted him with the customary, "Welcome aboard." She directed him towards his seat near the middle of the plane as she cheerily wished him a nice trip.

Jim found space in the overhead compartments for his carry-on bags and collapsed into his seat. As he buckled up he wondered if the steeplechase was over. Was he really, finally taking off for Cambodia? Would the light rain that was still falling delay this flight too? Would they taxi out to the runway and sit there for two hours without taking off? Was life all a cruel joke?

As the plane became airborne, Jim felt a surge of relief as none he'd ever felt before. He was on his way. He would get to Cambodia. He would return with Brendan. He knew more hurdles lay ahead, but at least for the next six hours he could relax and enjoy the flight to London. Wrong again.

15

Airborne
Monday, July 31, 2000

○ ○

My name is Kimberly. Tomorrow is my birthday. I'll be five years old. I already had one birthday party before my Dad left for Cambodia, but tomorrow I'm having another one with all my friends. We're gonna have real fun.

Jim gazed out the window as the plane quickly climbed above the cloud cover, soon reaching a cruising altitude of 34,000 feet. He knew that below the blanket of clouds there was a cold rain falling on an even colder ocean, but he somehow felt warm and secure. He didn't really understand why he or any other passenger should feel peaceful and safe while hurtling through the sky at 585 miles per hour in a thin metal cocoon, but why bother thinking about it?

The stress and angst of his frustrating night melted away with each passing minute. The cheery disposition of the flight attendants, a warm and reasonably satisfying omelet breakfast, and the showing of a movie, along with the steady drone of the jet engines gave Jim a good feeling and positive outlook. *This is more like it! Now I'm getting somewhere.*

Jim didn't know if last night's weather had any thing to do with it, but not all of the plane's seats were filled. As luck would have it, two of the adjacent seats were unoccupied, allowing him to lift the separating armrests and create a small "bed" for himself using a pillow and blankets provided by the flight attendants. Finding himself uninterested and unable to stay focused on a Steve Martin movie, Jim stretched out and tried to sleep. As tired as he was, he awoke after only an hour, his mind working overtime on details of the journey still to come. He dug out the travel packets that had been provided months earlier by the adoption agencies and began reviewing them again. Although they were very informative, and he was very happy to have them, Jim was struck again by all the warnings and cautions about everything from diseases, to food, to foreign government restrictions, to unique cultural norms.

Jim then turned his attention to the study of the Heathrow Airport layout shown at the back of the American Airlines magazine. He wanted to try to have a mental blueprint of where he would have to go once he landed to make his connection with the Thai Airways flight that he expected to board. Time would be limited after he landed and he didn't want to waste any of it wandering around the airport aimlessly. He was lost in his task when the cabin speakers crackled to life.

"Ladies and gentlemen," one of the flight attendants intoned urgently. "Are there any medical personnel on board, any doctors, nurses or medical assistants?"

Oh, oh. What's this all about? I don't like the sound of this.

After a brief moment of waiting, the worried voice again pierced the now hushed cabin.

"Ladies and gentlemen. We have a medical emergency. I ask again, do we have a doctor or any person with medical training on this flight? Please make yourself known to us immediately."

A medical emergency? Jeeze. Just my luck. What happens now? Oh please, God, not a new problem.

Suddenly, a well-dressed black man got up from his seat and walked quickly to the front of the plane where the chief flight attendant waited. Jim could not see what was going on at the front of the plane, and after a few minutes he went back to trying to plan his Heathrow strategy. But before long, the cabin speakers boomed to life with a male voice.

"Ladies and gentlemen, this is your captain speaking."

Oh, no. This can't be a good thing.

"We have a medical emergency on board. This will require us to make an unscheduled landing in Shannon, Ireland. I regret the inconvenience this may cause. We have no choice but to make an emergency landing."

Unbelievable! What else can go wrong? It's like a conspiracy to prevent me from getting to Cambodia.

As Jim stared blankly out the plane's window, the only thought that popped into his mind was a TV commercial featuring Cathy Lee Gifford standing on the deck of a luxury liner, having the time of her life, singing happily, "If they could see me now." *Oh, yeah. If they could see me now. What a great time I'm having on this trip. The time of my life. What a ball. Oh, well. Nothing I can do about it. Things like this must happen all the time on airlines. I've just got to relax. Go with the flow. If I miss the Thai Air flight I'm supposed to catch, I'll just have to find another.*

Jim felt the plane quickly bank and decelerate. They must have been close to Ireland and the pilot was forced to make a diving decent to Shannon Airport. Jim watched the wing flaps move back and forth as the engines roared and the plane vibrated. In minutes, they hurtled earthward through the thick cloud cover into a pouring rain. As they descended, Jim was struck by the green landscape below. As far as the eye could see, there was only lush, green rural countryside, the deepest green pastures he'd ever seen. And everywhere he looked, it appeared that the emerald blanket was dotted with flocks of white sheep. As the plane banked and circled for a landing, the green landscape with its white sheep extended right up to the edge of the airport runways.

The plane landed and taxied immediately to an isolated gate. The pilot announced that he would attempt to make the stopover as brief as possible. He explained that there were various protocols that must be followed for such an emergency landing and as soon as all the logs and forms were completed, they would be off to England. He did not provide any specifics about the medical emergency but did tell the passengers that they would be required to remain on the plane. Only the stricken passenger would be taken off the plane.

True to his word, the pilot announced the preparation for takeoff within an hour. Minutes later, they were airborne again. By now, dusk was settling over the British Isles and it was dark enough for the city lights to be lit by the time the plane circled London for a landing. Although Jim had flown into London a couple times before, his arrival had always been during early morning daylight. This was the first time he was flying in at night and the sight was nothing less than spectacular. As the pilot banked the plane low almost directly over the Thames River, London's famous landmarks were clearly visible, illuminated by powerful floodlights. *Magnificent. Simply magnificent. It's so picture perfect it's almost unreal.* Jim momentarily became a holiday tourist, staring in awe at the Tower of London, Tower Bridge, Westminster Abby, Big Ben, and the Houses of Parliament. Even Admiral Nelson's statue in Trafalgar Square was clearly visible. For just a minute, Jim felt like he was on vacation.

As Jim exited the jetway into the terminal, helpful American Airlines customer service personnel greeted passengers and asked if anyone desired assistance for flight connections. Knowing that he'd missed his Thai Air flight, Jim immediately responded that he did. An agent led Jim to a more secluded part of the gate area and sat at a computer terminal. Until Jim got accustomed to the word pronunciations, he had some difficulty understanding the man's thick British accent, especially because the agent spat out his words with machine gun speed.

The man listened patiently to Jim's quick explanation of his need to get to Phnom Penh, and then took a look at Jim's notepaper with the latest proposed itinerary. After a quick review of several computer screens, he told Jim that there were no other flights on Thai Air until the next day. But the good news was that his ticket to Cambodia would not cost five thousand dollars.

"You should get a ticket for about nine hundred fifty pounds. About one thousand five hundred American."

"A thousand five hundred dollars?"

"Yes."

"On Thai Airways?"

"That's correct. But you'll need to be up early in the morning and be first off at the ticket window," he said, as he confirmed the flight number and time of departure.

"Not a problem. That's fantastic. Just one more question, what do I do between now and then?"

The man looked at Jim's tired face and smiled. "I suspect you'll be needing a place to sleep." He fumbled briefly in the desk and produced vouchers that Jim could use for round trip transportation to and from the airport, and for meals and a three hundred dollar room at the nearby Fort Crest Hotel. All right!

Expressing his gratefulness to the American Airlines agent for all his assistance, Jim set off immediately to the baggage claim area to see if his luggage had made it to London. As he approached the baggage claim area, he encountered the well-dressed black man who had responded to the medical emergency on the flight from JFK. Jim's weariness was not overwhelming enough to kill his curiosity. He stopped and initiated a conversation with the man who turned out to be a doctor from Kenya. He told Jim an elderly male passenger with a history of heart ailments had actually died on the plane. In fact, the doctor guessed that the man had been dead for at least twenty minutes before the attendants realized that his "sleep" appeared to be a bit too deep.

Jim continued to the baggage claim, and to his great relief, he immediately spotted his luggage among the few bags and suitcases that remained to be picked up from his flight. He found the shuttle bus that would honor his voucher and boarded for the short drive to his hotel. One of the other passengers on the shuttle was a young girl on her way to San Diego for a death in the family. She had chosen to check all her luggage and all of it had been lost. The only possession she had besides the clothes on her back was her cell phone. *Well, I guess I'm not the only one getting dumped-on by the bird of paradise.*

Airborne Monday, July 31, 2000 99

◆ ◆ ◆

Despite a short night's sleep, Jan had gone to work Monday morning. After her early morning call from Jim and their agreement that he continue on, even with the prospect of a flight with a five thousand dollar price tag, she had shuttled Kimberly to the babysitter and gone off to her job. Although it was beyond imagination that anything else could go wrong, Jan had decided to call American Airlines during the late morning to check on the progress of Jim's flight to London. When she started getting the runaround from the airline about the status of the flight, she morphed into an assertive, unrelenting telemarketer on a mission. Her persistence led her through a maze of calls and transfers laced with the word "confidentiality", but finally brought the words "emergency landing" and "Shannon, Ireland". Only after much more heartbeat skipping questioning did the words "medical emergency" surface. American Airlines could not tell her more. Confidentiality. She spent the rest of the day trying to get some work done with a hopeful assumption that the medical emergency was not Jim. But she was worried sick.

Picking Kimberly up at the babysitter and rushing home in case Jim called, she waited in agony for the phone to ring. It was to be the last time that week that she would wish for the phone to ring. She spent the rest of the week hoping the phone would stop ringing as calls came in waves from concerned friends, relatives, and adoption agency social workers…and Jim. But on this night, she desperately willed the phone to ring until it did.

Three thousand miles away, across the Atlantic, Jim spotted an AT&T telephone near the hotel lobby on the way to his room. He dumped his luggage and ran to the phone.

"Jim?"

"Jan. You'll never guess where I am. I'm in London. I'm at a hotel in London," Jim said, thinking that Jan would not know about the emergency landing in Shannon. She would expect him to be winging his way on the Thai Air flight to Phnom Phen.

"London?" Jan said, realizing that Jim had missed the connection with Thai Air.

"Yes."

"What happened? The last information I was able to get from American Airlines was that your plane made an emergency landing in Shannon, Ireland."

"Yeah, some guy died on the plane. We only lost about an hour in Ireland, but that delay, along with the time for the additional landing and take-off, was enough to cause me to miss this afternoon's Thai Air connection in London."

Jim told Jan the whole story, from the flight attendant's announcement to his chance meeting of the Kenyan doctor on his way to the baggage claim carousels. He asked about Kimberly and inquired about whether his surprise birthday card had arrived. He asked about her birthday party, getting a bit confused about what day of the week it was. Jan reminded him that it was only Monday night and Kimberly's birthday party was to be the next day, on Tuesday. They talked about his new flight plans and how he now expected to get a ticket on Thai Airways the next day for only fifteen hundred dollars, and that his new route would now take him through Bangkok, Thailand. They talked about how tight the timeframe would now be to beat the adoption moratorium. They optimistically agreed that if nothing else went amiss, it could be done. Finally, they wished each other good night. There was no mushy talk of mutual affection. Love was understood.

Jim took a quick hot shower in the room's beautiful marble bathroom to make himself feel presentable. Vouchers in hand, he beat a path to the dinning room only to discover that the kitchen had closed for the night. Feeling beyond hunger anyway, he went to the hotel pub and ordered a glass of Bass Ale. Images of the Beatles, Herman's Hermits and other British rock groups flashed across a huge projection screen that covered half a wall as their music pulsated through surround sound speakers. Some other time, Jim would have enjoyed the pub atmosphere, but limping along on a total of two or three hours sleep during the past thirty-six hours, his quiet, beautiful hotel room beckoned him.

Back in his room, Jim dug into his bags and found the peanut butter crackers that Jan had packed with foresight. He also found the small half-pint bottle of Dewars Scotch that he'd stowed away for either a lonely celebratory toast or a desperation bracer. He poured himself an inch on the rocks, grabbed some crackers, and perched himself up in the huge bed, attempting to focus on his plans for the next day.

Too tired to think in depth about anything, he turned on the TV to discover a repeat of an old episode of the Dukes of Hazard. He sat in bed in a weary stupor, trying to make sense of the entire journey since leaving home for Providence Airport. He pictured himself standing alone in the rain at a deserted JFK terminal a little more than twelve hours earlier, feeling very much like a homeless person. Yet here he was tonight, luxuriating in a three hundred dollar London hotel room sipping his bootleg Dewars Scotch and munching on peanut butter crackers. Should be caviar, especially while watching something classy like the Dukes of Hazard. It was past midnight. He quickly fell into a deep sleep.

Across the Atlantic, a concerned Kimberly had listened intently as Jan recounted the tale of her Daddy's ordeal. As Jim slept, she said her prayers before going to bed. "God bless Mommy and Daddy. God bless Kimberly. And please God, don't let Daddy have a heart attack on the plane."

16

Tuesday, August 1, 2000

○ ○
My name is Kimberly. Today is my birthday. I'm so happy. While I'm having my birthday party, my Daddy is flying to Cambodia to get my baby brother.

Jim's hotel room telephone rang long before his tired body would have wanted. He had requested a very early wakeup call and the hotel desk complied. Groggy from a short night's sleep, Jim managed to mumble a polite thank you but told himself it was okay to rest just a few more minutes. Ten minutes later, the phone rang again.

"Good morning, sir. Just checking. Did we call you?"

"Yes, yes you did. Thank you."

"Sorry to disturb you. We just wanted to be sure we'd called."

"Thank you. Thank you very much for checking." *Pretty neat. A human snooze alarm system.* After he hung up, Jim decided he'd better get out of bed and get going. He just might have fallen back to sleep if they hadn't called back. He quickly shaved then jumped into a hot shower to fully wake himself and to get the blood flowing.

Even at the early hour, Jim found the breakfast dinning room already buzzing with activity. It was an elegant room, brightly lit with ornate chandeliers. By European standards, the hotel offered a first class buffet breakfast with all manner of breads and rolls, juices, fruit displays, cereals, sausage and ham, and pastries. Waiters fussed about the room replenishing water glasses and coffee cups at almost every sip, and clearing dishes as soon as they were empty. Jim smiled to himself as he sat in the upholstered chair. Feeling very privileged and pampered, he remembered all too vividly the previous day's Spartan coffee and bagel at the JFK food court.

After savoring breakfast for as long as he thought he could allow, Jim stopped by the front desk and checked out. He retrieved his bags from his room and jumped on the next shuttle bus. Although the distance from the hotel to Heathrow was only a few miles, the trip took much longer than Jim expected due to stops and passenger pickups at several hotels en route to the airport.

Jim arrived at Heathrow shortly before eight o'clock and couldn't believe his eyes. The airport terminals were already jammed with hundreds upon hundreds of people everywhere he looked. Tired and a bit disoriented from his lack of adequate sleep since leaving Massachusetts, Jim thought he was looking at end-of-the-weekend crowds, even though it was really Tuesday morning. But this was not just any ordinary Tuesday morning; it was Tuesday, August first. August is the main vacation month for many Europeans and they annually flock to highways, train stations and airports to begin the month-long "holiday" on the first of the month, regardless of the day of the week. Jim didn't know it, but he couldn't have picked a busier day all summer to be trying to get a flight anywhere in Europe.

Thinking he was supposed to check in through American Airlines, which had made the tentative reservation for him with Thai Airways, Jim joined the massive AA queue. The line snaked back and forth in an unbroken chain of shuffling humanity. Jim took his place at the rear and inched along with the throng of impatient travelers, juggling his backpack and carry-on diaper bag while kicking the duffle bag ahead and dragging the heavy Pullman behind. After a forty or fifty-minute eternity, Jim got his turn at the ticket counter. The agent looked at Jim's original British Air ticket and his latest printed itinerary while Jim briefly explained his dilemma and the sequence of events, including what he'd been told by the American agent upon his arrival at Heathrow the night before. The agent looked in the computer and told

Jim that he couldn't issue him a ticket for the Thai Air flight. There was indeed a tentative reservation for him that had been entered by the AA agent the night before, but Jim would need to go to Thai Airways to actually purchase the ticket. As he gave Jim general directions to the Thai Air terminal, which was a considerable distance away, Jim could feel himself getting anxious and tense again. Angry with himself for having wasted so much time in the American Airlines queue, Jim grabbed his bags and began to run, bump and excuse his way through the milling multitudes of travelers. He dodged and weaved his way past queue after queue for airlines he'd never heard of. In his haste and determination to get to the Thai Airlines terminal, he overshot his target. Stopping to ask directions, Jim was directed back a short way to a jumble of ticket counters that appeared to have the longest queue he'd seen yet that morning. His legs froze in place while his heart pounded its way up to his throat. The line seemed to stretch forever. *Oh no! I can't get at the back of that line. I'll never make the flight to Bangkok.*

Jim glanced around anxiously. He spotted what appeared to be a uniformed line greeter a short distance away from the busy counter with the long line. He went over to the lady and asked her innocently where he should line up for Thai Airways. He assumed she would direct him to the end of the long line whereupon he'd plead his case for urgent assistance to make his flight. Instead, she told him he was already in line for Thai Air just where he was standing. Jim looked in amazement at a counter with only one passenger and two ticket agents.

"This is it?"

"This is it."

"I can't believe it. Thank you, thank you."

Jim looked over at the long line that he thought was for Thai Air and could now plainly see that the queue was for another airline. He walked directly to the beckoning Thai Air ticket agent, smiled, and placed his now well-worn itinerary on the counter in front of her.

"I need to get to Phnom Penh," Jim said, beginning anew his brief explanation of his adoption journey, recounting the story of missed flights, and telling her of the American Airlines agent's instructions from the night before.

"Yes, I see your name here," she said as she made the first of several inquiries on her computer.

Jim watched her reactions as her fingers hammered the keyboard. The occasional faint frown on her face as she studied the computer screens did not bode well. As the minutes ticked by, Jim began to think there was a problem with the tentative reservation that had been made by the American Airlines agent. When the ticket agent called the supervisor over for consultation, his level of apprehension heightened. *Oh God, not again. Now what?*

The supervisor looked up from the computer screen and said, "Mr. Pacenka, we can indeed provide you with a seat on the next flight to Bangkok, but it will be a Royal First Class seat that will cost five thousand fifty dollars. The flight from Bangkok to Phnom Penh will cost approximately an additional thousand dollars."

"Give me a break! Can't you do something to help me out here?" Jim blurted in shock, expecting the fifteen hundred dollar ticket that the American Airlines agent had told him about. His mind was racing. *Six thousand bucks! The whole round trip fare from Providence to Phnom Penh that Lotus Travel had booked was only eleven hundred dollars. Now they want six grand just to get from London to Phnom Penh? I've got six thousand cash but I can't use that. I need it for the adoption fees over there. Will my credit card be able to take the hit? We've been putting a lot of charges on that card during the past month. I don't even know what limit I've got on the card. I've got the backup card we never use. That card should be okay.*

"I'm sorry sir," the agent said. "The coach seats are fully booked on this flight. The only seat available is in Royal First Class, and we are not allowed to discount walk-up fares at the airport ticket counter. All discounted fares are sold only through travel agents or our web site, usually far in advance of a flight."

"Yes, yes. I understand," Jim replied, appreciating the futility of the moment.

Jim handed his credit card to the agent, trying to convince himself he should at least be happy about getting a seat on the plane. Then he glanced at the clock on the wall behind the ticked counter and realized how much of the morning had already slipped away. It was ten minutes past eleven and the flight was scheduled to leave at noon.

Regardless of her repeated data entry into the computer, the agent could not obtain an approval code for the transaction. Finally, she asked Jim for a different credit card. *What if I didn't have another card? Does everyone in the world carry more than one credit card? Jeez, good thing I brought the extra card for backup.* Jim handed the agent his L. L. Bean Credit Card. *Well, this ought to earn us a bunch of shopping credits!*

After initial difficulty in getting an approval with the second credit card, the two Thai Air agents eventually discovered the proper entry codes and the ticket was issued.

"Am I going to have time to make this flight?" Jim asked with a worried look at the clock.

"Don't worry Mr. Pacenka, you will definitely be able to make the flight. Your bags please."

Jim passed his large backpack, the duffle bag and Pullman over to them. Since there was no conveyor belt behind the counter, Jim wondered how the bags would get to the plane to be loaded on time. *Oh sure, that would be the final kicker of this trip. I pay an extra six thousand dollars to get to Phnom Penh and voila, no luggage.* As at JFK, he comforted himself with the thought that he had all the documents he needed, a change of underwear and some extra clothing in his carry-on. The agent assured him his luggage would arrive safely with him and gave him directions to his gate, which was on an upper level.

Jim walked briskly to the escalator, feeling emotionally drained and physically weary even though the day was only a few hours old. Lack of sufficient sleep for the past two days, along with constant tension and anxiety-provoking obstacles, were creating a severe drain on Jim's energy reservoir. But determined to reach his goal, Jim bounded up the escalator and took a right down the long concourse that would lead him to gate fifty-five and his flight to Bangkok. As soon as he rounded the corner, Jim spotted the long lines at the security checkpoint. He took a place in what he hoped was the fastest moving line. Shortly, a well-dressed man with a Thai Airways logo on his jacket came by and spotted the special color-coded ticket Jim held in his hand. He greeted Jim, insisted on carrying Jim's bag, and immediately escorted him through a short line at the side of the security check area. Giving Jim the "sir" treatment the entire way, he led Jim directly to his gate. *Royal First Class treatment. All right!*

Since it was now only about fifteen minutes before flight time, the gate waiting area was nearly deserted as most of the passengers had already boarded the huge aircraft that was partially visible through the terminal windows. *Holy smoley, the thing looks like Air Force One!*

Thai Air service personnel validated Jim's boarding pass and whisked him through the short jetway onto the cavernous airplane. A waiting female flight attendant, wearing a beautiful crimson dress with a silk scarf, greeted Jim cordially. She glanced at his boarding pass, and then led him to a staircase spiraling to an upper deck. As Jim went up the staircase, he looked down at the hundreds of passengers in economy class. The rows of seats seemed to stretch to infinity. With Thai music raining down from the overhead speakers, Jim began to feel he was entering a world quite foreign to him in every possible way.

The opulent Royal Class cabin was like nothing that he'd ever seen on an airplane. Huge, plush seats that could recline into full beds were arranged spaciously in rows of two. Each seat had an individualized storage compartment and a personal TV screen for viewing a selection of movies. Large rectangular windows provided picture window viewing as compared to the usual tiny port windows at regular jetliner seats. Colorful oriental tapestries adorned the walls of the cabin. As Jim took his seat and began studying a personal control panel of buttons, he was immediately greeted by a smiling attendant who handed him a menu, and asked if he would like a drink. Jim's head was already spinning so he passed on the drink and began studying the meal options.

As the plane took off, the passenger in the seat next to Jim introduced himself and offered to help with the menu selection as he drained a complimentary scotch on the rocks. His name was Terry and he was a native New Yorker who lived in Thailand. He worked for a company that produced helicopter equipment and accessories. *Must have one sweet job to be able to afford to fly around in Royal Class.*

Terry had learned the basics of the Thai language. He reviewed the many menu selections with Jim, from salads to main courses and wine selections. *So this is how the other half live! Incredible. Wonder what the folks downstairs in coach are going to eat?* Jim decided to pass on the Tom Yang Kung and the Kaeng Massaman Kai. He chose a salad and a pork entrée that he hoped would be similar to something he'd once had in a local Thai restaurant. Terry laughed at Jim's reaction to a plate of various appetizers that soon appeared with one of the attendants. Most of the items on the plate looked a bit too exotic for Jim's taste. Terry talked him into trying something that looked like a Thai version of tiny Swedish meatballs made with sausage. Jim was glad he only took a couple to try because they were like little balls of shoe leather slathered in a less than appetizing sauce. When the meals arrived, they were served on fine chinaware with beautiful silverware place settings. Cuvee Des Roys champagne was available with the meal for those who wished to give their palates a Royal Class treatment. *How will I ever be able to fly coach again?*

It turned out that Terry loved to drink and talk. He wasted no time getting into both. He told Jim how he'd gotten drafted for the Vietnam War in the sixties. After basic training, he'd been offered the opportunity to go to officer training and flight school. He jumped at the chance and was trained as a helicopter pilot. After training, he spent the better part of a year transporting troops and freight before getting trained to fly a Cobra combat helicopter.

The more Terry talked, the more he drank. Top shelf scotch, compliments of Thai Air. The more he drank, the more he talked. He rambled on about combat troop drug usage in Vietnam and about a fellow copter pilot who wanted to go in business with Terry when they were discharged. But Terry opted to go to work for an oil company, flying helicopters back and forth to oilrigs in the Gulf of Mexico. He was just getting bored with that job when his buddy from Vietnam called him about an opportunity with his company if Terry was available to go live in Thailand. Terry took the job, and eventually took a Thai bride as well. *This guy's lived one heck of an interesting life. Wonder how much of what he's telling me is true and how much of it is just booze talking? At the rate he's throwing those glasses of scotch down, by the time we get to Bangkok, he'll be able to fly without a plane.*

After a while, Terry tired of talking about himself and concentrated on downing more scotch. For a while, Jim busied himself with another review of some of the material in the adoption travel kit. Although he felt as if suspended in a dream world, he reminded himself that he really was now on his way to Phnom Penh, and in another two days, he'd be on return flights with baby Brendan in his arms.

The flight was a long one, about thirteen hours. After Jim exhausted his attention span on the travel kit, he decided to enjoy the luxuries of flying Royal Class with Thai Air. A Video Walkman gave him access to an onboard video library that included several first-run movies, some classic films, and a choice of a ballet, music, or sports video. Jim sampled some of the videos but was not inclined to view any of them from beginning to end. He became more fascinated with a large flat screen digital display on the wall of the cabin that showed the minute-by-minute progress of the flight, including altitude, air speed and the unbelievably frigid temperature outside the aircraft. The silhouette of a tiny aircraft was superimposed on a global map and watching its progress toward Bangkok gave Jim a refresher course in world geography. He watched in awe as the plane traversed Europe, cruised over the Black Sea and Turkey, brushed the border of Iraq, and crossed over

Iran, Afghanistan and Pakistan. As the plane soared over the Himalayans at 47,000 feet, Jim briefly wondered what would happen if they crashed-landed in the mountains. He seemed to remember having once read an article or seen a TV story about a Himalayan crash-landing and how some people had survived the crash only to face the incredible challenge of staying alive near the wreckage to await a hoped-for rescue. *Had they resorted to cannibalism? Had some survived? Was it a real story or fiction? Whatever. Not much chance of survival if this baby splats into Everest or one of its sister peaks.*

As the plane streaked through the sky into darkness, Jim noticed that Terry either fell asleep or passed out from trying to drink the plane's scotch supply dry. Fatigue and the effects of a couple gin and tonics induced Jim into joining Terry and most of the other passengers in trying to get some sleep. Since the Royal Class cabin was above and forward of the engines, it was as quiet as an empty cathedral. Jim pressed the button to reline the seat, and within a minute, he too had joined the airborne sleeping village.

Jim only slept for a couple hours. He didn't know why. Perhaps he had too much on his mind. His body wanted to shut down, but his mind refused. He got up to stretch and walked to the rest room, which he discovered was also first class. In addition to being much larger than typical aircraft restrooms, there were gleaming toilet fixtures, linen towels, sparkling mirrors and a selection of perfumes and colognes to give the passenger that pampered feeling. *I could get used to this.*

One by one, the thirteen hours drifted by like passing clouds beneath the big jet's wake. Just before dawn, the jumbo jet began its decent and the lights of Bangkok appeared in the distance like a mirage in a dark desert. As the plane approached the city, Jim was surprised by what he saw below. He expected Bangkok to be some sort of small urban oasis in the jungle. Instead, he saw a huge metropolitan sprawl, complete with a massive spider web system of highways and expressways leading into, out, and around the city. From high above, Bangkok looked like any large American city at night. Streetlights outlined city blocks and avenues, seemingly laid out in orderly Asian versions of urban planning. Lighted skyscrapers and city parks stood proudly in testimony of the ability of a Third World country to build modern cities. And as the plane swooped in for a landing, although the airport appeared small, it looked to be as modern as any.

While the plane taxied to its gate, passengers began the ritual of gathering their belongings, eager to exit the plane and get on to whatever lay ahead. Children made sure to grab their souvenir toys and gifts from Thai Air, while female passengers clutched the Madam Pompadour orchids that they were given to brighten their flight. Jim checked around his seat to be certain he was leaving nothing behind, and then packed away the neat gift toiletry kit from Thai Air. Kimberly would make proud use of it on sleepovers with her friends in the year to come.

Jim exchanged farewell wishes with a very tipsy Terry. *Good luck to him if he's going to work today.* Jim stepped out of the air-conditioned plane onto the jetway and immediately slammed into a wall of the most oppressive heat he'd ever experienced. *Hello Thailand.*

17

Wednesday Morning, August 2, 2000

o o o o o o o o o o o o o o o o o o o o o o o o o o o
This morning my name is Saveth. This afternoon it will be Brendan Saveth. I will be a Lucky Baby.

While Jim was arriving in Bangkok early Wednesday morning, halfway around the world in Massachusetts, it was still early Tuesday evening. Jan was feeling as exhausted and emotionally drained as Jim, perhaps more so. At least Jim knew where he was.

"Hi. No, nothing's new," Jan said into the phone for the umpteenth time in the past few hours. "I haven't heard any more since Jim called from London. If all went well for him today, he should be getting to Bangkok soon. He might even be already there. After that, he's only got a short flight to Phnom Penh."

All the relatives, friends, and adoption agency workers meant well, and Jan appreciated their concern and support, but she did wish the phone would stop ringing for a while. "At this point, no news is good news," she said. Then after a pause, "Yes, of course. I'll let you know as soon as I hear anything. Thanks."

After the call, Jan went back to tidying up after a hectic day with a handful of pre-schoolers. Between telephone calls, Tuesday had been Kimberly's birthday, and the day had included an outing to the movie theater along with the usual fun and games and birthday cake. Actually, the birthday celebration had begun the night before. Jan had stopped by a neighbor's house to pick up one of Kimberly's friends for a birthday sleepover. The neighbor wasn't feeling well and almost passed out while they talked. Jan ended up taking both of the neighbor's children home with her.

In between the happy bedlam with the children, the constant incoming phone calls, and the out-going calls Jan kept making to try to locate Jim, she had managed to make contact with American Airlines. She was determined to get American to assume financial liability for the missed China Air flights that led to the several thousand dollar cost for the Thai Airways flights from London to Phnom Penh. Her first call to American on Monday had left her very encouraged after a representative assured her that the problem would be easily be resolved in her favor. By Tuesday, bureaucratic buck-passing among different departments had taken over and it was no longer a given that the additional costs for Jim's travel would be borne by American. Not only was nothing settled that day, but Jan would spend the rest of the week on the phone seeking resolution.

Jan's biggest frustration on Tuesday was not knowing Jim's whereabouts nor knowing his final arrival time in Phnom Penh. She had notified the adoption agency that Jim's original itinerary was no longer valid. She needed to know Jim's new arrival time so that West Coast International could arrange to have Jim's driver waiting for him at the airport. More importantly, with the moratorium deadline rapidly approaching, the agency also needed to know Jim's arrival time. Agency representatives in Phnom Penh needed to make the necessary arrangements and appointments with Cambodian officials and the American Embassy for the adoption process. Time zone considerations added to the communication problem. Jan had to constantly remind herself that the west coast was three hours behind her while Jim was eleven hours ahead.

Tiring from playing the "where in the world is Jim?" game, Jan decided to send an email to him via the Sunway Hotel where he was scheduled to stay while in Phnom Penh. She made the message brief and to the point, "Lost track of you. Airlines can't or won't tell me where you are. Please call me. Love, Jan."

To round out her hectic day, by early evening, Jan discovered Kimberly was coming down with a summer virus. By her bedtime, Kimberly was running a temperature of 102 degrees. *Happy birthday!* It was close to 2:00 am by the time Jan went to bed wondering if more normal days lay ahead…and wondering where Jim was.

◆   ◆   ◆

Around the time Jan was discovering that Kimberly was getting sick, Jim was arriving at Bangkok Airport. It was about 6:00 pm on Tuesday for Jan, but 5:00 am on Wednesday for Jim. He knew the flight to Phnom Penh was scheduled for 9:30 am, so he had plenty of time to make the connection. After a bit of wandering around trying to figure out the location of the gate for his next flight, Jim approached a Thai Airways representative for information. She told him he had quite a long wait, and seeing that he was holding a Royal Class ticket, she directed him to the "Royal Orchid First Class Lounge" located on the northern departure concourse.

A beautiful young hostess greeted Jim at the entrance to the lounge. She was one of several Thai attendants in the lounge dressed in striking bright blue-red suits or dresses. After checking Jim's ticket to be sure he should be granted use of the Royal Lounge, she invited him to make use of the many amenities provided. Seeing her computer terminal, Jim asked if she could check on his flight to see if it was on schedule.

"Mr. Pacenka," she answered in an assuring tone, "you need not be concerned about your flight. Please enjoy our Royal Tulip Lounge. We will notify you when it is time for you to depart."

There was a huge, elegant dining area that had sectional seating with beautiful wood railings dividers. Carpeting and tapestries blended perfectly with wood accents to emphasize the look of luxury. In the center of the dining area was an inviting buffet of common and exotic fruits, so artistically arranged, that it was near impossible to pass by without sampling. Mounds of rolls, croissants, and pastries beckoned as well. A beverage counter offered a variety of juices, tea and fresh brewed coffee, along with espresso and cappuccino. And for the traveler who preferred to drink lunch, a hostess stood ready to pour a glass of fine wine, mix a cocktail with top shelf liquors, or stir a perfect martini. Hoping to boost his energy and stay alert, Jim passed on the tempting bar and opted for pastry and juice. He sat at a brilliantly polished table in one of the central dinning nooks and took in the sights around him as he slowly savored his royal treats.

Later, Jim "toured" the rest of the Royal Lounge. He walked past businessmen dressed in tailored suits who sipped martinis as they worked with their laptop computers at beautiful desks with leather chairs. He passed another area of the lounge that had private rooms with couches and electric massage chairs where families or individual travelers could rest and relieve stress. Jim located the men's restroom, which, like the one on the plane, had everything a man needed to groom himself into looking like a presentable traveler. Jim took advantage of the amenities. He shaved, washed, and changed into fresh clothes. Though still tired from minimal sleep in two and a half days, Jim somehow felt refreshed and eager to get on to Phnom Penh.

Since Jim had never flown as a Thai Royal Executive passenger before, he was unaware of the special treatment he was due to receive. Had he waited patiently for notification by the Royal Lounge hostess as instructed, he would have been whisked to his flight just minutes prior to departure and avoided the crowd scene for boarding. Not knowing this, Jim left the lounge and made his way to the boarding gate for his flight, having to pass through a security screening area once again.

At the gate area, Jim discovered there was no direct boarding of the plane via a jetway from the terminal. Instead, he found himself in the midst of a bumping, jostling crowd, jockeying for position to board "cattle trucks" to be driven to the plane that was parked on the tarmac.

Stepping outside to board the truck was once again like walking into a sauna. The heat was immediate and oppressive. The driver of the truck that Jim boarded seemed unsure of the correct plane and circled several of the parked planes before stopping at one of them. Jim joined the other passengers in scampering off the truck and streaming towards the small roll-up stairs to the plane. There were two entrances to the plane and Jim went to the front steps.

Unlike the huge transcontinental Boeing jetliner with the luxurious upper deck that had taken Jim from London to Bangkok, this was a small regional type jet and the Royal Class ticket meant only that Jim was seated in the first row. An Asian man, dressed very much like a businessman on his way to a meeting, took the seat beside Jim. He was an uncharacteristically large man compared to all the other Asian men Jim had seen thus far, but he was very pleasant and sociable.

The take-off came quickly after boarding and Jim soon found himself viewing a never-ending carpet of green foliage below, broken here and there by ponds and watery terrain. He tried to compare the topography to anything he'd seen before and the closest similarity he could think of was the Florida Everglades. Occasionally he'd spot a small village with a few thatched huts, but no large buildings or anything that looked like a town or city. And no highways, just narrow dirt roads near the villages.

The friendly Asian businessman seated next to Jim spoke English capably and engaged Jim in conversation. When he inquired about the nature of Jim's travel to Phnom Penh, his simple response to Jim's reply about an adoption was, "Lucky baby, lucky baby," a common Cambodian response that Jim was to hear again and again. He went on to apologize to Jim about the deplorable condition of the country, as if he was personally responsible for decades of political upheaval and for dictator Pol Pot's 1970's genocide of three million Cambodians. And if the political turbulence and corrupt governments weren't enough of a curse, Cambodia was entering the twenty-first century additionally crippled by an epidemic of aids and tuberculosis at the same time as the country's fertility rate topped most of its Southeast Asian neighbors. Most Cambodians, Jim learned, were born into a life of poverty and squalor that is beyond the imagination of most Americans, and venturing out into the Cambodian countryside surrounding its cities is often like stepping back into the thirteenth century. It was all a bit depressing, but it made Jim feel better than ever that he was on his way to take one more child away from a potential living hell to the relative paradise that was America. He understood the simple words, "lucky baby".

Soon came the announcement that the plane was approaching Phnom Penh, and Jim glanced eagerly out the window. As the city came into view, its appearance had no comparison to the approach to Bangkok. Although Phnom Penh is a bustling capital city of over a million inhabitants, from the plane, it looked to Jim like a small American city, surrounded by forests and vegetation. It did not look metropolitan, nor did it look like what he expected a capital city to look like.

When the plane circled low to land at Pochentong Airport, Jim's view from the air was a section of the city that looked old and run down. The plane bumped down in a hard landing, and as it taxied down the runway, Jim was unimpressed by the small airport that also seemed to be in a deteriorating state. He could see broken sections of old fencing surrounding the airport, and maintenance buildings with doors hanging off the hinges. Over the fences Jim saw peasants working in the fields, dressed in black from head to toe despite the burning sun.

The plane came to a stop on the tarmac some distance from the terminal and passengers were once again treated to a blast of Cambodia's humid heat as they stepped down the stairs from the plane. The passengers streamed off the plane and darted like a school of fish towards the small, flat terminal building. Jim was near the front of the crowd, following behind an armed guard who led the parade of passengers from the plane to the terminal. As Jim trudged along behind the guard, his exhaustion and the heat made him feel as if he might collapse right there on the hot tarmac. "Just don't fall, just don't fall," he kept telling himself. He had to concentrate intently just to get his legs to take each step forward. He felt immediate relief as he stepped into the air-conditioned terminal.

Uniformed guards, dressed in military brown, were everywhere. The passengers faced a row of perhaps two dozen male and female military personnel sitting low behind a long counter-top. Passengers were instructed to hand over their passports to the first military person at the long counter and then to walk along a white line painted on the floor. Jim followed instructions and walked slowly along the white line, watching in amused fascination as each military bureaucrat looked at the passport, looked at Jim, sometimes mumbled something, and then passed the passport to the next head peering over the counter at Jim. After the first five or six hand-offs, Jim began to get self-conscious and thought it better to avoid eye contact with the examiners, so he walked slowly along the white line looking ahead as innocently as possible. *Jeeze, this is weird. Why do I feel uncomfortable? My passport's fine. I haven't done anything wrong. Why do these people look at me and make me feel that I look suspicious to them? I'm not a damn criminal. I'm just here to adopt a baby. Must be the military uniforms. Man, this feels creepy.*

At the end of the line of military clerks, the passports piled up in a stack. Passengers then had to wait for their name to be called out to step forward to the last clerk who collected twenty dollars for a one-month visa. Passengers strained to listen carefully to every name called out, trying to decipher their names out of the mangled syllables that were shouted with a Khmer accent by the clerk. Jim stepped forward eagerly when he heard "Phakenka!" called out. The pronunciation was close and Jim felt lucky after watching the frowns and question marks on the faces of many passengers who weren't sure just who was being called to the counter.

Jim quickly paid his twenty dollars and walked away from the long counter thinking he was now free to go claim his luggage. He soon found himself at a blocked passageway to the baggage claim area. Two more military types stood beside tables, effectively blocking the way.

One of the men took Jim's passport and visa, looked at it, and began questioning Jim,

"Why in Cambodia?"

"Just tourism," Jim lied, remembering the instructions in the adoption agency travel kits. The kits warned adoptive parents to always respond to such questions with "tourist" as the answer; never state that adoption was the reason for the visit to Cambodia. Jim never understood the logic of the recommendation.

"What you will be doing?"

"Just visiting the country, traveling," Jim mumbled.

The man looked at Jim. Jim looked back.

"You are here to adopt baby?" It was more of a statement than a question.

"Yes, yes I am," Jim answered immediately, thinking it unwise to lie. *To hell with the travel kits. These people must know why I'm here. Big Brother is watching! I'll just get into trouble lying.*

"Lucky baby, lucky baby. You do a good thing," the man said softly.

Jim felt a flood of relief as the man returned the passport and visa and moved aside to allow Jim to continue to the baggage claim area. Spotting a men's restroom, Jim sidetracked for a quick stop and was surprised to find such an updated and clean facility. In fact, Jim was surprised by the modern equipment and excellent condition of everything inside the small airport. The interior stood in stark contrast to the first impression he had from the outside view on the runway.

Walking briskly out of the restroom, Jim passed right by the small, recessed baggage claim area. He soon found himself walking past a customs table staffed with more soldiers. He nodded at them and continued walking a short way before realizing that he was exiting the building. He turned around, walked back to the customs table, nodded again and said simply, "Luggage?" The soldiers pointed to the direction Jim had come. He looked back, spotted the baggage claim, and wondered how he could have walked right by without seeing it. *Boy, I must be more tired than I realize.*

Minutes dragged by, and Jim began to worry that his luggage had not made it to Phnom Penh on his flight. Each bag that appeared on the conveyor gave false hope. After ten to fifteen minutes that felt like an hour, Jim's luggage seemed to magically appear on the conveyor. He grabbed his bags and returned to his "friends" at the customs table. As he waited his turn, he watched as some passengers were singled out for searches in which three or four soldiers would unzip the bags and search through every square inch of the luggage. When Jim stepped up for his turn, the soldiers simply waved him through.

Jim stepped through the doors and walked out into the crushing heat. He felt a bit disassociated, as if he were walking around dazed in a dream. He shook it off and glanced around. He knew his next task was to locate the personal driver that was to have been arranged for him through the adoption agency. Adoptive parents arriving in Phnom Penh all hired drivers at a cost of thirty dollars per day. A driver served as an on-call chauffeur, a porter, a tour guide, an interpreter, and an instant Cambodian ally. The thirty dollars per day was fantastic pay for the Cambodian driver and a bargain for the American adoptive parent.

Jim saw a huge crowd of people standing behind what New Englanders would call a snow fence. They were obviously awaiting the arrival of relatives and friends. It was only then that it dawned on Jim how small the airport terminal really was. The passenger pick-up and waiting area was an outdoor fenced-in pen under the shade of a few palm trees!

Jim stepped off the curbing and walked down a dirt pathway towards the waiting crowd. As he walked slowly along the fence, he spotted a man holding up a sign with the word "Pacenka" at the top, and the word "Saveth" printed beneath. Jim maneuvered as close as he could to where the man was standing, pointed at the sign, and said, "You're my driver." The man looked at Jim, and knowing that he'd have trouble pronouncing "Pacenka", said to Jim, "Saveth?"

"Yes, Saveth," Jim replied.

While this exchange with the sign-carrier transpired over the fence, Jim became aware of another Cambodian man standing next to him.

"You're late," the man said to Jim.

"No kidding," Jim replied, knowing he was a day late but thankful the driver was still there.

Jim learned that the man who approached him was a Cambodian nicknamed "Octopus" who was to have been Jim's driver. Because of Jim's uncertain and delayed arrival, Octopus had committed to another assignment, but he obtained another driver for Jim, named Artchu, the man with the sign on the other side of the fence.

Artchu met Jim at the end of the fence, took his bags, and led him to his car that was parked nearby. His car was a maroon Honda Civic in mint condition, in and out. The car, Jim learned, was Artchu's ticket to good paydays as a driver, and he took great pride in keeping his maroon livelihood shiny and immaculately clean. Jim got into the car and Artchu drove to a female attendant at the entrance to the lot. It appeared to Jim that Artchu paid a parking fee and a tip to the attendant for allowing him to park close to the end of the pathway where he'd met Jim. After paying the attendant, Artchu drove out of the parking lot and started driving down one of the roads leading away from the airport towards the countryside.

"We go to orphanage?" said Artchu in a tone that assumed a positive response.

Jim struggled to think clearly. He thought he should first check into the hotel, unload his luggage, and then go shopping for some things he needed for the baby as well as to buy gifts for the orphanage.

"Which way is the hotel?" Jim asked, thinking the hotel must be along the way to the orphanage.

"That way," Artchu replied, pointing over his shoulder in the opposite direction they were traveling.

"I need to go to the hotel first," Jim told Artchu, who agreeably turned the car around and headed into downtown Phnom Penh.

The ride into the city was interesting. Some might even describe it as exciting. The road was fairly wide, a highway of sorts, but roughly paved. It reminded Jim of a New England coastal highway with sand and dirt blowing around everywhere, and tall weeds growing alongside the edge of the road. The highway was filled with cars, mopeds and bicycles, all oblivious to lanes and directions. Everyone went wherever they wished, weaving and darting in front of each other at will. From above it must have looked like water bugs zipping helter-skelter over a puddle of water.

Before long, Artchu had managed to arrive safely in the heart of the city and pulled up in front of the Sunway Hotel. From the outside, at least, it looked like a beautiful modern hotel. Sunway staff swarmed out to the car to carry Jim's bags and escort him inside to register. Artchu stood by his shiny maroon Honda as Jim took a deep breath and allowed himself to feel good about the moment. Finally, it…was…all…really…happening. Within the hour, he'd be at the orphanage and Saveth would be more than a picture in his wallet. Soon, he would be holding his son in his arms.

18

Wednesday Afternoon, August 2, 2000

o o o o o o o o o o o o o o o o o o o o o o o o o o o o
My name is Brendan Saveth. My daddy has come to get me. I am going home.

Jim was immediately impressed with the Sunway Hotel staff tripping over one another to assist him with registration and to deliver his luggage to his room. He soon realized they were all vying for tips, but it felt good to be so pampered. The cleanliness and modern elegance of the lobby carried through to the beautiful brass-trimmed mirrors in the elevator. A computerized keycard gave access to his spacious and well-appointed room, complete with a well-stocked wet bar. Upon entering the room, the porter instructed Jim to slip the keycard into a slot on the wall. As he did, electric power to the room's lighting was activated, as was power to the television. Jim would discover that when he pulled the card out of the slot to leave the room, all the power except the air conditioner shut down for automatic energy conservation. *Pretty neat.*

Jim quickly gathered the things he wanted to take to the orphanage and packed them in the diaper bag. He dug into his six thousand dollar stash of cash in his money belts and took out the amounts he thought he'd need for the afternoon. When he walked out the lobby doors, Artchu stood waiting patiently beside his shiny Honda. As the car pulled away from the hotel, Jim told Artchu he needed to make a stop at a local market to pick up a few things on the way to the Cham Chao Orphanage.

"Take me to the Lucky Market, okay?" Jim said. That was the name of a local market where Jan and Jim had been advised to shop.

"No, not there," Artchu replied. "I take you to other market."

"But why not go to the Lucky Market. I was told it was a good one," Jim protested.

"I take you to better market. You like. You see," said Artchu, ignoring Jim's request.

In a few minutes, they arrived at a small market that reminded Jim of an old American A&P Supermarket of decades past. The exterior of the market had seen better days. Artchu drove up onto the sidewalk and parked close to the building. He got out, locked his car, and handed money to two well-dressed young men loitering near the market's entrance. They became instant security guards for Artchu's prized Honda.

Artchu accompanied Jim inside. The market had about a half dozen aisles that were about fifty feet long. The shelves were fully stocked with everything an American would expect to find in a small market back home. Jim first walked by the produce section and was amazed to see broccoli, celery, tomatoes and other common vegetables and fruits stacked alongside more the exotic produce that he expected to see. He was also pleasantly surprised to find an extensive baby-supply section containing name brand products that would be found in a market back home. He spotted two large cans of the brand of powdered baby formula that had been recommended and grabbed them. The price for the formula at a local market in Massachusetts was over twenty dollars per can. In Artchu's market, they were priced at five dollars each. Jim picked up a supply of disposable diapers and discovered that these too were only about a quarter of the price he would pay back home.

The market had everything, even liquor at very attractive prices. Jim spotted Johnny Walker Black for six dollars and Bombay Blue Sapphire Gin for only five dollars and fifty cents. He was severely tempted to grab a couple bottles at that price but he resisted the urge when he thought of how difficult it already was to juggle all his heavy bags. And on the return, he would also have Brendan. *Forget the booze.*

Jim selected some small toys, and after consulting Artchu, he also bought a huge bag of rice to give to the orphanage. Jim paid for his purchases with readily accepted American money and received his change in local currency, the Cambodian riel.

As Artchu drove out of the city, he went into his tour guide mode and pointed out various important buildings to Jim, such as the Royal Palace and the National Museum. He did not comment on the occasional women and children beggars who positioned themselves strategically throughout the city. Many were visibly malnourished and missing limbs, tragic victims of land mines and other ravages of war.

After they drove around a rotary a few miles down the road, Artchu made a right turn. The small highway immediately turned into a muddy dirt road pockmarked with large puddles of water that sometimes camouflaged deep potholes. Off to the side, peasants could be seen wading through rice paddies. Artchu gingerly steered his Honda through the muddy obstacle course, trying to go around as many of the large holes as he could, but he was often forced to drive the car slowly through the deep, water-filled craters in the road. Jim wondered how long it would take Artchu to clean his sparkling Honda after this trip.

Thankfully, after rocking and rolling through about a half mile of mud holes, a complex of white buildings came into view, surrounded by a wall with a gate. Artchu pointed to the large white structure at the center of the complex and said simply, "Orphanage". He stopped in front of the large wrought iron gate and tooted his horn. A caretaker appeared and opened the gate. As Artchu drove up to the large building, a river of squealing children poured out of the main entrance. When Jim got out of the car, several of the children ran towards him, perhaps hoping today would be their lucky day.

"Who here for, who here for?" the children yelled excitedly.

"Saveth," Jim replied, "I'm here for Saveth."

"Saveth, Saveth," a handsome young boy yelled as he ran back into the building.

"Yea, yea, Saveth, Saveth," the other children cheered.

After a few awkward moments, a woman holding a baby appeared in the doorway. Jim instantly recognized her as Saveth's nanny from the pictures that had been sent to Jan and Jim from the orphanage. Without expression or emotion, she walked slowly to Jim and handed Saveth to him.

Jim stood in the blazing hot sun with a peaceful Saveth in his arms. His mind was numb and fuzzy from days of deprived sleep and wakeful tension. He struggled to bring this poignant moment into focus. A squadron of thoughts, some happy, some sad, dived-bombed in waves, but one impacted first and foremost. *I wish Jan were here. God how I wish Jan could be with me to share this incredible experience.* But half a world away, it was two hours past midnight in Massachusetts and Jan was just falling into a troubled sleep, having gone to bed still not knowing where Jim was.

Jim looked at the cute little bundle dressed in green and blue, kissed him on the cheek, and said to the nanny, "Thank you." Then, after a couple of awkward minutes, he turned to Artchu and asked, "What do we do now?"

"We go to office."

They removed their shoes at the door and entered the pleasingly bright and clean orphanage. Jim followed the nanny to an interior office where an older, stone-faced, matronly woman joined them. She sat silently throughout the visit, never expressing anything other than a nod of the head when accepting the gifts Jim had brought for the orphanage. In addition to the large bag of rice and toys that he'd procured at the market in Phnom Penh, Jim had also brought some antibacterial hand lotions and baby clothing for the orphanage. He also gave $100 to the nanny. Everyone seemed pleased.

As they prepared to leave, the nanny gave Jim a bottle of prepared formula. He thanked her and asked naively, "How will I know when he's hungry and wants to be fed, or needs changing?"

"He tell you. He cry. You know."

Jim asked if it would be permissible to take some pictures before he left. An affirmative answer sent him scurrying back to Artchu's car to retrieve his camera. He was led into a large room where numerous baby baskets hung from the ceiling rafters. He asked which basket had been Saveth's, placed him in the basket and took his picture. Outside, he took a couple pictures of the orphanage and had Artchu take pictures of him with the nanny and Saveth.

As they drove down the dirt road to return to the highway, Jim looked at an old house they had passed on the way in. Several small naked children were playing in a large puddle of water in front of the house. He was tempted to ask Artchu to stop so he could get out and take a picture until he spotted a mean-looking dog with large teeth growling menacingly at the small Honda crawling past through the potholes. Jim decided to skip the picture.

Back on the highway, Jim's attention alternated from smiling gazes at the son he was now calling Brendan to head-turning observations of the chaotic driving habits of the locals. He was fascinated by the passing parade of cars, mopeds, old bicycles that looked like WW II vintage, and an occasional businessman humming along on a shiny Kawasaki. Artchu told him that in spite of the helter-skelter, devil-may-care driving habits of the locals, accidents were not as frequent as one might expect due to the relatively low speeds of the traffic. That was a good thing, he said, because no one carried accident insurance. If there was an accident, they somehow just settled up among themselves.

Jim was most amused by the multitude of mopeds buzzing along like angry hornets. Many of the mopeds carried a passenger. Some went by with three people crushed together, holding on for dear life. Once, almost like a circus act, a moped labored by carrying a family of five! But the prizewinner, Jim thought, was a moped bouncing along with two men, the passenger somehow balancing himself while holding a huge pane of glass in outstretched arms.

Artchu wanted to take Jim sightseeing on the return to the hotel. Jim told the driver he was very tired and had much to do with what remained of the day. Perhaps tomorrow there would be some time for sight seeing, but today he must return directly to the hotel.

As they neared the Sunway, Jim noticed a small park adjacent to the hotel. It was beautifully landscaped around a huge clock built into the hillside. Back at the hotel, Jim went directly to his room, took off all his clothing and tossed them into a trash bag and did the same for Brendan. He filled the large bathroom sink with warm water and bathed Brendan from head to toe, looking for any signs of disease. Brendan gave Jim a studied look throughout the process, but the agreeable four-month-old baby did not protest. Jim toweled Brendan dry and then covered him with scabies lotion. He put the baby in the car seat and the two of them took curious measure of each other for a few minutes. After seeing that Brendan was content in the seat, Jim jumped into the shower.

The hot water pelting his back felt magically restorative and he luxuriated in its massaging effect as he allowed a special shampoo for lice to soak his hair for ten minutes. After the shower, feeling clean and refreshed, Jim covered himself with scabies lotion. Jim was starting to feel like someone with an obsessive-compulsive personality disorder, but the clothing disposal, the bathing, the shampooing, and the lotion application were all high priority recommendations in the travel kits provided by the adoption agencies. They warned of serious potential health consequences if personal hygiene instructions weren't followed scrupulously.

After looking over messages and flyers that had been slipped under his door, Jim dressed himself and Brendan and took the beautiful mirrored elevator ride down to the lobby. He planned to find the West Coast International staff located in the hotel to get the final adoption processing done. One of his messages stated that he needed to meet with Dr. Nancy Hendrie, the American doctor who oversaw the American adoptions from the Cham Chao Orphanage. She would complete a final brief exam of Brendan and conduct the final paper processing for the adoption.

The West Coast International staffer chided Jim good-naturedly.

"You're late, a day late."

"You got that right, but you have no idea what I had to go through to get here," Jim replied, ready to begin his tale of woe.

"I know, I know. Just kidding. The news about all your misadventures reached us. Glad you made it okay."

"I had a message to see Dr. Hendrie."

"Well, unfortunately, we're not going to be able to do that just now. She's going to be tied up for a while with some embassy folks and another group of parents. We've set up a new meeting time at 7:00 pm for your group."

Jim looked at his watch. It was 5:30 pm. This would be a good time to send an email to Jan. It would be waiting for her when she awoke in a couple hours. He went to the business office where two beautiful young hotel employees dressed in bright red hotel uniforms greeted him cordially. He explained that he'd like to send an email. They pointed to two computers that were available for hotel guests to send email at the rate of four dollars for fifteen minutes. A man was just leaving one of the computers. One of the young women brought Jim to the computer, made a few keystrokes and told Jim he was ready to go. He confessed to her that he never used email and needed a bit of help. She set the screen up for him and told him all he had to do was type his message.

As she walked away, Jim began to type but immediately pressed a wrong key that sent the cursor into hiding. Jim called her back for help. She showed him how to get the cursor back and left again. Jim no sooner began typing a second time and the cursor moved to the wrong place. He started to hit the backspace button and got himself into more trouble. He called for help again.

"You keep type like this, you spend many time four dollar," she said smiling.

"I know. I'm not very good at this. Do you think you could type the message for me? It's not very long." Jim waved the piece of paper that he'd used in his hotel room to scribble a brief message to Jan.

"Okay, you tell me," she said and sat at the keyboard. She typed as fast as Jim could speak the words. He told Jan he finally made it to Phnom Penh and was at the hotel. He told her how he had already gone to the orphanage to get Brendan, how adorable he was and how good a baby he was being. He told her all was well and that he'd be meeting with Dr. Hendrie in about an hour and a half.

While Jim was involved with the secretary sending the email, the other young woman lifted Brendan gently out of his car seat. As she hugged and rocked him in her arms, he responded with loving eyes and sweet smiles.

"Happy baby, happy baby," the secretary said. "Lucky baby. Lucky, happy baby," she repeated several times as Brendan responded with more smiles.

When Jim dictated his closing, "I love you, I miss you," the young woman stopped typing and stood up.

Looking shyly at Jim, she said, "I no do that. That personal. You must type, then click send."

Jim managed to type the last words and send the message successfully. He thanked the young woman for her help. She smiled.

With hunger now making an aggressive statement in his stomach, Jim went from the business office directly to the restaurant. Along the way, he saw directional signs for conference rooms, a beauty parlor, a business center, a fitness room and spa, and a babysitting facility. Jim guessed that it would cost at least three or four times as much as he was paying to stay at a comparable hotel in Boston,

The restaurant reminded Jim of the elegant Royal Lounge in Bangkok. The décor was all orange and maroon tones with expensive-looking draperies on the windows and exquisite tapestries on the walls.

A long, attractive buffet table, complete with ice sculptures and fruit suspended in ice blocks beckoned invitingly. The buffet, with a choice of soups and main courses, offered an easy alternative to ordering from the full menu. While Brendan slept contently in his car seat, Jim enjoyed a chicken and rice entrée then attacked the artistically arranged fruit table. He would have been content to linger for a while, savoring a cup of coffee after the meal, but seven o'clock was upon him and he left quickly to retrieve the adoption paperwork in his room before making a beeline for the meeting with Dr. Hendrie. Once again, he found himself playing a losing game of beat the clock.

19

Wednesday Night, August 2, 2000

○ ○
My name is Kimberly. Today I'm going to talk to my Daddy in Cambodia on the telephone. Mommy promised.

Jim arrived at the meeting room a few minutes late. He quickly discovered that Dr. Hendrie had begun the group meeting promptly at seven o'clock, causing him to miss some of her preliminary instructions. He sheepishly took a vacant seat among the eleven other adoptive parents who were seated around the large oval table.

Dr. Hendrie was pleasant but business-like. Years of experience with jet-lagged, anxious adults suffering from situational attention-deficit disorders had apparently caused her to develop a pedantic schoolmarm approach to these group-processing sessions. A stack of forms was placed before each adoptive parent, but everyone was strictly admonished to stay with the group.

"Listen to everything I say. Don't skip ahead. Don't fill out any entry until I say to. I'll tell you what to fill in on each line of each form and what to leave blank. Please pay attention. If the forms are not completed properly, you will fail to obtain a visa for your child. Do you understand that? Without a visa, you will not be able to take your child back to the United States."

Jim and the others felt like first grade students being spoon-fed word-by-word instructions by a no-nonsense nun in a parochial school. And of course, when weary adults are treated like children, they begin to take on the role. The group became giddy, laughing at themselves and at each other when less than genius-level questions were addressed to Dr. Hendrie, or whenever a frequent "oops" was heard at the table. Predictably, the frivolous atmosphere led to a vicious cycle of erroneous entries leading to more banter, leading to more erroneous entries. A persevering and patient Dr. Hendrie delivered mock scoldings, and the parents began to act like participants on the TV reality show "Survivors", taking turns voting each other off the "island" with each transgression.

It took close to an hour and a half to finish the form-filling exercise. Despite the group's lighthearted approach to the task, they all understood its importance. They knew that Dr. Hendrie's expertise was invaluable to them. When she barked the command to write "unknown" in a blank space, they knew better than to write anything else. Dr. Hendrie knew all the answers needed to get past the bureaucrats handing out approval stamps and visas.

As soon as they were done, Dr. Hendrie instructed them to go to a conference room on one of the upper floors of the hotel where they would join other adoptive parents for a final "meeting". Time had come for the last cash payment to West Coast International. This closing adoption service fee was ostensibly a contribution to the Cambodian orphanage system that funded Cham Chao and several other facilities. Unfortunately, it may also have been part of the reason that Cambodian adoption practices were being accused of corruption, or that some Cambodian adoptions were being called "baby-laundering". Very likely, the cash donations may have contributed to INS suspicions about the supply of Cambodian orphans, and perhaps helped generate the investigation that was creating the moratorium of American adoptions. But to Jim and the other parents in that room, the cash payment was simply a modest and reasonable fee in the net cost of realizing their adoption dreams.

Jim entered the small conference room to find dozens of adults and children already there. Although Jim was making the journey solo, as were a half dozen other men he'd met in the lobby, most of the adoptive parents came as couples. Many were sufficiently affluent to travel to Cambodia as entire families with children in tow. Compared to Jim, who was trying to fly in and out as fast as he could, some of the parents turned the adoption journey into weeklong vacations in Cambodia. Some created extended vacations with two or three week stopovers in other countries on their way home.

The conference room was not only too small for the assembled group, it was puzzlingly bare except for a table with handout materials at the front of the room. Lacking chairs to sit on, parents and children staked out space on the floor, which thankfully was covered by plush, beautiful carpeting. Until Dr. Hendrie called the meeting to order, chaos reigned. Adults climbed over each other to get to the front of the room to collect informational material they'd lost or missed along the way. Children scampered about at will, hopscotching over outstretched legs and around or over sleeping and crying babies. Brendan was a sleeper, peacefully so, until a "friendly" child came over to "play" by sticking her finger up Brendan's nose. Her mother thought that was just so cute. Jim whispered a suggestion to the little girl that she seek out another nose to play with.

When Jim allowed himself to think about it, he was feeling exhausted, but on that count, he did not feel alone. One quick look around the room gave evidence of many dark-circled eyes, drooping eyelids, and non-stop yawns. For his part, Brendan had taken the afternoon and evening in stride without apparent fear of the strange new faces and environment. Jim, carrying bottles of formula like six-guns in the large leg pockets of his fatigue-style pants, became quick-draw McGraw whenever Brendan so much as whimpered. With an instantly provided nipple to suck on, a full tummy to go, and a clean diaper after, Brendan was the Gerber baby picture of contentment.

Everyone tried to be comfortable on the floor, but it was not like being at the beach. The room was cramped and hot, and as the meeting wore on, there was no gentle breeze to dissipate the pervasive stench coming from non-stop diaper changes around the room. It wasn't long before the conference room stunk like a ripe outhouse, and all the scented baby powder in the world couldn't cover it up. Jim wondered if the room would be filled with executives for a breakfast meeting the next morning. *Hope they like a lingering aroma of diaper bouquets with their croissants!*

Dr. Hendrie lectured the group on a variety of subjects, most of which had been covered in the travel kits provided by the adoption agencies. Predictably, she stressed health issues.

"All your children have been exposed to tuberculosis," she said slowly in a loud voice, emphasizing each word so she could be heard over the noise of the children and the shushing by their parents. "When you get home, you must get them examined. Immediately. They must have a TB test. And then six months later, they must be tested again. Do you understand? They must be tested again. I don't care what your doctor tells you, do this."

When Dr. Hendrie finished her presentation, parents queued near the front of the room to make their $3,500 contributions to the orphanage system. A young lady from West Coast International collected the cash. As Jim waited his turn, he watched in disbelief at the casual way the young lady collected the money. She made no attempt to count the wads of cash to be sure there was $3,500, and she showed no obvious concern about the condition of the bills. *I'll be darned! I killed myself running around Worcester like a nut for five days trying to find new, uncirculated bills because they said that's what we had to have, no exceptions. No creases, no folds, no bank marks. For crying out loud, the way she's grabbing those stacks of bills, she doesn't seem to care if they were picked out of the gutter.*

As the line shortened and the stack of cash grew, a man from New York standing in front of Jim turned to him and said, "Holy shit, have you ever seen such a pile of cash? Must be close to seventy-five grand there. You'd think they'd be worried about someone barging in here to grab the dough and run."

"You'd think," Jim agreed.

As the man reached the young woman and handed her his $3,500, he said to her, "Say, aren't you worried about walking around Phnom Penh with all that cash? The stuff we read before coming over here put the fear of God in us about flashing cash around like that. Do you need one of us to go with you for protection?"

"Thanks, but it's not necessary. There's nothing to worry about in a hotel like this. I'm just going as far as the hotel vault tonight." Unknown to the parents, the young lady was usually accompanied by discreet Cambodian bodyguards as she moved around Phnom Penh.

◆　　◆　　◆

Jim was silently grateful when the parents' meeting finally ended. He retreated quickly from the crush of people, the noise and the smell. His hotel room was a tranquil oasis. He had just finished changing Brendan's diaper and was eyeing the wet bar when the phone rang.

"Jim! Jim, I finally reached you. How are you doing?"

The words came through choppy, the voice sounding distant with a slight echo. But it didn't matter.

"Jan?"

"Oh Jim, it's so good to hear your voice."

"Man, you don't know how good it is to hear yours too. It's been a haul, but I made it. You got my email?"

"Yes, this is my second attempt to reach you since I read it this morning. I was dying to talk to you. It's been crazy back here. The phone's been ringing off the wall. Everyone was worried about you and wanted to know how you were doing. I kept having to tell them that I didn't know, that I hadn't been able to talk to you since your stopover in London."

"Well, the worst is over. Tomorrow I go to the American Embassy, finish the final paperwork, and get the visa for Brendan. The next day, I fly home."

"I can't wait till you're back home, safe and sound."

"Me too, but Jan, you're gonna love Brendan. He's such a good baby, and he's beautiful. Everywhere I go, people fuss over him and say how cute he is. I'm looking at him right now. He's sitting here in his car seat looking back up at me."

"Oh good, good. But to be honest Jim, I've hardly thought about him since you left because I've just been so worried about where you were and how you were holding up. So tell me more, tell me all about Brendan."

Jim spent several minutes describing every detail about Brendan and his natural good humor. After he felt confident that he'd at least temporarily satisfied all of Jan's inquisitiveness about Brendan, Jim turned his attention to the little voice he could hear in the background.

"How's Kimberly? Did she get my birthday card?"

"Yes. It made her happy. She's right here and wants to talk to you."

"Okay, put her on."

"Daddy, Daddy!"

"Hey Kimberly! How's my little girl?"

Kimberly, always a joyful chatterbox, ordinarily would have talked up a storm, staying on the phone forever, talking about everything and nothing. Thankfully, for the family budget, Kimberly soon got frustrated with the sound delay of round-the-world telephone communications. She just couldn't develop the patience to wait in dead silence for her words to reach Jim and for his to get back to her, so they both kept talking over each other instead of to each other. But that didn't stop her from insisting that a couple of her friends get on the phone to say hello to her Daddy in "Cambowdeeya". The conversations were disjointed to say the least. Nevertheless, they stayed on long enough to help make it a $275 call. Jan and Jim's phone bill for that week would eventually total $879.

"What's all the commotion I hear in the background?" Jim asked Jan when Kimberly passed the phone back to her.

"Joe just dropped by to help me set up the new baby crib before you get back. He brought his kids and your mother. Kim's got two of her friends over here, so with seven kids and three adults, this place is rocking."

"Sure sounds it."

"Your mother and Joe say hello and want me to tell you how relieved they are to hear you're okay."

"Yeah, tell 'em I'm fine. Nothin' to worry about now…even though I feel like I've been to hell and back just to get here. But, everything's going good since I got here. It's almost over. Before you know it, I'll be back home with Brendan."

"I can't wait."

They chatted a few more minutes about the trip, the heat in Phnom Penh, about how good and adorable Brendan was, and about the flight arrangements for the return journey before saying a reluctant goodbye.

Jan hung up the phone, heaved a sigh of relief, and returned full speed ahead to her hectic day. Jim tucked Brendan into bed, desperately hoping for a blissful night's sleep. He was so focused on collapsing into bed, he never heard the loud 11:00 pm "bong, bong, bong" from the nearby hillside clock that had caught his eye earlier in the day.

20

Thursday Morning, August 3, 2000

○ ○

My name is Brendan Saveth. Today will be a busy day for my new Daddy and me. I will be a good baby. He will be happy with me. All will be well. Buddha smiles upon me.

Sleep, blessed sleep, was not meant to be. All night long, every hour on the hour…bong…bong…bong. Even worse, the big hillside clock wasn't the only problem. Jim's room was at the back of the hotel. Loud voices speaking in Khmer, a radio blasting Cambodian music, and crashing and banging sounds jumped right through Jim's closed thermo pane windows as if invited. Nighttime hotel deliveries and maintenance crews. Since the noise kept Jim awake most of the night, he couldn't blame Brendan for occasionally waking and fussing. Crash, bang…bong…bong…bong.

 Jim managed only a couple of hours of on and off sleep during the night. Rather than lie in bed trying to fall back asleep, he took to sporadically getting up to busy himself with little tasks as quietly as he could so as not to wake Brendan. The noisy deliverymen and the hourly gonging of the clock took care of that. It was probably around one o'clock in the morning when Jim boiled water in the coffee maker and sterilized nipples for the next day's feedings. Around 2:30 am he sorted through all the paperwork needed for Brendan's visa application and checked to be sure he had everything. And it may have been around 4:00 am when he decided to read some of the handouts he picked up at Dr. Hendrie's meetings.

By 7:00 am Jim gave up all hope of additional sleep. He decided to get up to shave and shower, even though he only planned to go to the Embassy at 10:00 am. He washed, dressed and fed Brendan before preparing a couple of four-ounce bottles of formula for his six-shooter pockets. Then it was off to the dinning room.

Everything at the elaborate breakfast buffet looked appetizing to Jim. He placed Brendan's car seat in a visible location at one of the booths where he could keep him in sight as he attacked the buffet tables. After grabbing a large orange juice and coffee, Jim headed to the omelet station where he directed the cook to throw in mushrooms, onions, peppers, and the kitchen sink. He got hungrier by the second as he watched it sizzle and sniffed its tantalizing aroma. After devouring the omelet and a couple croissants layered with butter, Jim went back for another omelet. Then it was on to the fruit table, another artistic masterpiece that seemed to display every fruit known to man.

As Jim sat back and slowly savored another cup of coffee, he glanced around the room absentmindedly, observing the mix of businessmen and adoptive parents. His moment of peace was soon shattered as an older couple with a crying baby came in and sat at the adjacent booth. Jim remembered meeting them briefly in the lobby and thought they were from Iowa. Jim figured them to be pushing sixty, perhaps older...too old for regular adoptions by American standards. From their haggard faces, it looked as if their night had been even more trying than his.

The husband, with thinning salt and pepper hair and a gray beard, had the look of a stern professor, stiff and formal. His face was screaming unhappiness. The wife looked as if she had just stepped out of a Norman Rockwell portrait of a 1940's grandmother serving Thanksgiving turkey. Her ankle-length dress was old-fashioned and her silver-gray hair was pulled back tight against her scalp into a fist-sized bun at the back of her small round head. She seemed to have incredible patience with the crying baby as she tried to eat breakfast.

"Darn it Mary, can't you shut that baby up?" the husband hissed between mouthfuls of pancakes and sausage.

The patient wife ignored the husband and continued to rock the baby in her arms, talking in soothing tones, looking lovingly at the child they'd traveled halfway around the world to adopt. The baby kept crying. The husband threw his napkin on the table and stormed out of the dinning room. The wife paid no attention and continued to rock the baby. The baby paid no attention and continued to cry. Jim looked at a peaceful Brendan, thanked his lucky stars for such a good baby, and decided he'd had enough coffee.

Back in the hotel room, Brendan's diaper sent a clear message to Jim's nose that it was time for another diaper change. The diaper change went well, but the aftermath created a little excitement and a learning experience for Jim. He left Brendan lying on his back on the bed as he stepped across the room to toss the soiled diaper in the trash bucket. In the split of a second, as Jim turned back to the bed, Brendan decided to show off his developing motor skills by flipping himself over and rolling off the bed. Jim could see it all happening as if in slow motion but he was ten helpless feet away when Brendan hit the floor. Fortunately, Brendan landed softly and harmlessly on the plush carpeting. His brief, tiny whimper as Jim picked him up indicated he was unhurt, but extremely surprised by his freefall. Jim cuddled him, kissed him and checked him as best he could for an injury. The immediate return of Brendan's winsome smile gave Jim instant relief.

"Hey big fella, that was some trick you just pulled on me. Good thing you didn't get hurt. And good thing nobody was here to see it. Instead of letting me adopt you, they'd probably send me packing. You're a lucky baby and I'm a lucky guy."

Jim went down to the lobby a few minutes before ten o'clock and chatted with some of the other adoptive parents who were waiting for their drivers or just killing time. He met a couple of parents from Massachusetts, including one who lived in Gardner, about an hour away from Jim's home. The lady from Iowa walked in with her crying baby. The husband was nowhere in sight.

Jim spotted Artchu pulling up in front of the Sunway, right on time as usual. Jim excused himself and walked to the main entrance, forgetting that he'd been a beneficiary of the hotel's efficient air conditioning system since the prior afternoon. He stepped out the door and once again slammed into the wall of heat he'd been introduced to when he stepped off the plane. *Holy cow, it must be a hundred degrees out here and it's only ten o'clock. What's it gonna be like by this afternoon after it really heats up? Thank god Artchu's car's got AC. Get me outta here!*

As Artchu circled away from the Sunway, he drove by the house-size hillside clock that had gonged its hourly eye-opening salutation all night long. Jim briefly reflected on how innocent and serene the impressive clock looked at 10:05 am, then his attention was quickly drawn to the chaotic traffic of Phnom Penh. Cars, mopeds and bicycles careened around each other and shot through intersections at will. No one seemed to pay any attention to the traffic lights. *This is insane! These people make Boston drivers look like gold star graduates of driving academies.*

After Artchu had driven a short way from the center of town, Jim was shocked to see a large Red Cross building that looked as if it had been gutted by fire. The widows were all broken and the building appeared to be riddled with bullet holes.

"What happened, Red Cross have a fire?" Jim asked Artchu.

"Yes, a fire," he replied. Then after a pause, he added, "Khmer Rouge."

"Oh."

"No one come back to fix. Just put fence around building."

Not long after they passed the Red Cross building, Artchu turned left down a narrow road that was more like an alleyway than a street. He soon spotted and squeezed into the only parking spot in sight.

Besides being reliable and prompt, this guy's a hell of a driver. Some people could have spent a week trying to back their car into that spot.

"Okay, I take care Saveth. You go," Artchu told Jim, pointing to a compound of buildings protected by a high gate and small guardhouse. Several brown-uniformed guards milled around the gate. Small in stature with baggy pants and little hats, to Jim, they looked more like young boys playing soldier than the real thing. But then he looked at their rifles and thought about the Red Cross building they'd just passed.

"You go," Artchu repeated. "You tell guards you here to adopt baby."

"That's it?"

"Yes. Say you here to adopt baby."

As Jim walked toward the gate, he felt totally out of place, out of synch. The narrow street was lined with dirty, yellowed stucco houses and buildings that had once been white. The street seemed to be closing in on him. He could sense that "alone against the world" feeling creeping back in. He didn't know why, so he told himself to walk straight and look confident as he approached the gate.

He announced to the guards that he needed to visit the embassy because he was adopting a baby. They waved him in with barely a glance. No more than fifty paces into the compound, he found himself at a second gate with a female uniformed guard.

"I'm here for an adoption," Jim said.

"You go there," the female guard said, pointing to the entrance of a chain-link passageway covered by a wooden roof. The hundred-foot-long breezeway was lined on both sides with benches. Cambodians sat crowded together, shaded from the blazing sun, waiting for their turn to approach the embassy building.

"There?"

"Yes. You go. You go to front of line."

"Past all the people waiting?"

"You here to adopt baby. You go first," the guard ordered.

Jim began to walk through the passageway as instructed, feeling very self-conscious and guilty about passing ahead of all the waiting people. There must have been a hundred of them, maybe two hundred. For the first few steps, he tried not to look directly at any of the people, stealing peripheral glances as he walked by. Some were destitute looking and some were well dressed, but they all looked old to Jim, real old. Each one looked up at him as he walked past and he could feel their eyes following him. The faces showed no expression, but Jim felt certain they must feel resentment to see him walking straight to the front of the line. He stopped pretending that he wasn't seeing them and began to nod to them and smile apologetically, mumbling a stupid-sounding "thank you" or "excuse me" here and there as he walked past. He didn't know how long they had already been sitting in the heat, nor how much longer that day they'd continue to sit in the heat waiting their turn, but he knew he felt uncomfortable as hell for being so privileged as to be allowed to pass them all by.

Reaching the building, he found two more guards positioned in front of a large bulletproof glass window with a small open slit for communication. It reminded him of a movie ticket booth. An old Cambodian man stood at the window talking to a man seated inside. As Jim reached the guards, he told them he was there to adopt. One guard immediately grabbed the old man's shoulder to push him aside from the window. Jim, more embarrassed than ever, protested diplomatically.

"No, no, no. That's okay. Please, let him finish." Jim didn't want to offend the guards or get started on the wrong foot with the guy behind the window, but he resented the treatment the old man was getting.

The guard looked at the man behind the glass and asked, "He done?"

The man behind the glass just smiled and nodded as he passed some papers to the old man through the window slot. The old man collected the papers, bowed a couple times, and moved off to the side without a word.

Jim slipped his papers through the slot, the documents that he'd prepared at Dr. Hendrie's "survivor island" group session the prior night. The man took the papers, shuffled through them briefly, and then looked at Jim.

"You have money?"

"Money?"

"For medical exam fee and visa fee."

"Oh, yes, yes," Jim answered quickly as he dug into his pocket. He counted out $126 and passed the money through the slot. The man counted the money, stamped some of the papers, and handed Jim a receipt.

"You keep receipt. You need to proof you pay visa."

Jim took what the man passed back to him and turned to leave. As he did, he discovered the American couple from Gardner, Massachusetts standing right behind him.

"How ya doing?" the man asked.

"Good, good," Jim replied, "I guess I'm all set. How about you?"

"Fine. Can you believe all this?" he asked with an upturn of his eyebrows.

"Jeeze, I know. It's something else."

"I feel awful," the wife whispered. "They made us go in front of all these poor people."

"I know, but that's what the guards said to do."

The couple shrugged and stepped up to the window and Jim started back through the long passageway. He felt compelled to nod left and right as he walked, saying, "thank you, thank you" to the expressionless Cambodians waiting patiently in the brutal heat.

Arriving back at the car, Jim wanted to grab his camera and go back to have a picture taken of himself and Brendan with the guards. Artchu told him that the guards would not allow that. Jim figured the driver knew what he was talking about so he directed Artchu to drive him to the airport. Jim wanted to check on his flights and reconfirm his reservations for the next day. After his trials and tribulations getting to Cambodia, he wanted to leave nothing to chance for his return home.

21

Thursday Afternoon, August 3, 2000

o o o o o o o o o o o o o o o o o o o o o o o o o o o
My name is Brendan Saveth. I am having such fun traveling around Phnom Penh with my new daddy. I like him a lot and I can tell he likes me.

After initially going to the wrong Thai Airways terminal, they found the correct reservation location and Jim verified his flights home. In addition to confirming the connecting flight segments with multiple airlines, Jim's biggest concern was confirming Brendan's seat. The Thai Air agent tried pooh-poohing Jim's concern. Remembering all too clearly the call from Jan's friend recounting how they had paid for, but never got the seat for their baby on the return from Cambodia, Jim would allow no quick dismissal of his concern.

"Look," Jim insisted politely but forcefully, "I paid $600 for Brendan's seat, and I want to be sure that his seat reservation is right there next to mine on all the flights. There's no way I'm going to hold my child in my lap to travel halfway around the world."

Hearing the determination in Jim's voice, the agent reluctantly but dutifully pecked away on her keyboard for several minutes before reassuring him that indeed, Brendan's seat was secure on all flight segments. Jim thanked her and went away satisfied that he'd done all he could to be sure his flights and seats were confirmed. The next item on his agenda was laundry.

Artchu drove Jim back into Phnom Penh and assured him he would take him to a reputable laundry. Soon, Artchu deftly maneuvered his prized Honda down a side street that seemed no wider than an average-sized room. Small, dirty decrepit stores and shops lined the street, and stooped old men and women shuffled along a cracked and uneven sidewalk. Jim tried to hide his skepticism with a poker face as Artchu pulled up in front of a small storefront with a large dirty window. *You got to be kidding me! This is the laundry? I'll never be able to wear my clothes again.*

"Artchu, you sure this place is okay?"

"Sure okay."

"Will I get my clothes back?"

"No problem."

Jim had trusted Artchu from the gitgo, but he couldn't warm up to a Cambodian ghetto laundry. His nose curled and his skin crawled just looking at the laundry entrance. But he needed to get some clothes washed for the return trip home. He had already thrown the first day's clothes away. *What the hell.*

"Okay, do it."

Artchu opened his trunk, took out the large plastic bag that Jim had stuffed with clothes and disappeared into the laundry. Within a minute, he was back. Jim gave Artchu his camera so the driver could take a souvenir picture standing in front of the laundry…surrounded by several curious locals.

"Okay, where to now?"

"Take me to see the palace," Jim answered without hesitation, "I want to take some pictures of the Royal Palace."

Jim had glanced at his watch while Artchu was in the laundry and saw that it was already past eleven. His time in Phnom Penh was quickly coming to an end and he doubted that he'd ever be back. He wanted to be a tourist for at least an hour or two. Somewhere in his interactions with some of the other adoptive parents at the hotel, he'd been told that the Royal Palace was worth a look. Artchu agreed.

As they drove along, they passed a large field where a carnival was operating, fenced off with flimsy chicken wire. Besides being quite small, the Ferris Wheel and other amusement rides looked ready for the junkyard. *No way I'd ever get on one of those rides or let my kids get on either. That Ferris Wheel looks like it should be condemned before it collapses. I wonder how the locals can afford to take their kids there anyway?*

Artchu turned onto a large boulevard and soon arrived in the vicinity of the Royal Palace. Built in 1866 at the broads of the Tonle Sap (Great Lake) River, the palace was currently occupied by King Norodom Sihanouk. The impressive pagoda style structure was part of a large Royal Palace compound with several structures on manicured grounds. One of the buildings was the so-called Silver Pagoda, made up of 5,000 silver tiles and housing hundreds of Royal gifts and treasures, including a solid gold Buddha encrusted with more than 9,000 diamonds.

Traffic in the area was light and Artchu had no problem pulling over to give Jim various views of the Royal Palace and many opportunities for photos. The driver parked the car and they walked around to the river side of the palace. Although Jim could feel the mid-day heat rising, a cooling breeze from the river made the temperature tolerable. They walked over to a high river wall where Jim gazed down into the muddiest water he'd ever seen. He supposed that the silt and mud carried along by the flowing water was good for rice paddies and other agriculture along the riverbanks, but it certainly made for an ugly river next to a beautiful palace.

Returning to the car, Artchu, now the tour guide, tried to persuade Jim to visit the Killing Fields of Choeung Ek where the Khmer Rouge slaughtered 17,000 Cambodians, just nine miles from the center of Phnom Penh. Jim checked his watch and saw it was past noon and he had to be back to the hotel for a 2:00 pm meeting with U.S. Embassy staff. Moreover, the gruesome thought of viewing the 8,000 skulls on display at the Killing Fields Memorial didn't strike him as the type of highlight that would enrich his memory of his brief adoption journey to Cambodia.

"Let's go back to the hotel," Jim told Artchu, wanting to have time for a leisurely lunch before the meeting.

"We stop for shopping?"

"Shopping?"

"Yes. Nice shop. Good souvenirs."

"Okay, quick stop," Jim answered, remembering that he'd been told that adoptive parents would be steered to shopping at stores offering crafts and products made by handicapped war victims.

Artchu drove down another narrow street, but unlike the laundry area, the buildings here were all well maintained. A white stucco wall and tall palm trees lined the road. The driver soon pulled into a small courtyard fronting a large three-story building that looked like a home converted into a store. The courtyard was filled with bushes covered with huge exotic flowers that Jim assumed were some type of orchids.

The ground floor of the building had large clean windows and Jim was impressed with the neat and clean appearance of the store as he entered. An elderly American woman, a retiree, who helped Cambodians run the store, greeted him. With Artchu tending to Brendan, Jim wandered freely through the three floors of the store, a mini-version of an American department store. The variety of products and gift items was amazing and even included a Christmas shop with decorations, ornaments and large artificial Christmas trees. He wondered how an American tourist would haul a large Christmas tree halfway around the world to get it home. Better yet, how to explain that the Christmas tree was purchased in a Buddhist country?

Jim had entered the store thinking he'd just blow quickly through the place and get out of there. But the more he walked around, the more interested he became. He thought there would be just a lot of useless crafts and junk trinkets, but he found beautiful products and gifts at every turn, all attractively inexpensive. One of the items that he agonized over for several minutes was a spectacular silk quilt that was priced at just $35. He'd have willingly paid $350. It was that handsome. The problem was size. It was too large to fold up and pack into his luggage to take home and the store didn't have shipping services. It pained Jim to walk away from the quilt without buying it, but he bought a gorgeous, small embroidered picture as a consolation prize.

Jim was the lone shopper in the store. As he wandered around, the heat and his sleep deprivation made him feel a bit lightheaded and dreamlike. With the large ceiling fans circling slowly above and a smiling female Cambodian face peering at him from behind one of the counters, Jim began to fancy himself as living a scene from Casablanca or some similar movie with an exotic locale.

By the time he left the store, Jim, the reluctant shopper, had purchased the silk tapestry, a beautifully embroidered tee shirt, a Christmas ornament, a silver ring, some silver charms for Kimberly and Jan, and a few other small gifts. When he stepped out into the warm sun, he marveled again at the spectacular flowering bushes and the beautiful birds darting in and out of the branches. He felt good about himself. Everything he'd purchased was a bargain, but every dollar he spent was assisting the handicapped war victims.

Arriving at the Sunway, Jim invited Artchu into the hotel for lunch. They ordered cold sodas and Jim ordered a sandwich, but he couldn't talk his driver into anything to eat. Artchu finished his drink and left as other adoptive parents entered to have lunch. They all traded information about their morning escapades. Jim was glad that he not only passed up the Killing Fields, but also the National Library, another popular tourist stop. Apparently, annoying and aggressive beggars surrounding the Library frightened many of the young American children who accompanied their parents for a visit. The one regret Jim did have was his lack of time for a trip to Angkor Wat, a celebrated Cambodian temple a couple hours away from Phnom Penh. *Ah well, gotta face it, I didn't come here for a vacation.*

♦ ♦ ♦

After a quick trip back to his room to change and feed Brendan, Jim went back down to the Sunway's main lobby to join other parents getting prepped by Dr. Hendrie and her assistant from West Coast International. The parents had been told to meet in the lobby at 2:00 pm, but each had to wait his or her turn to be called into a small room adjacent to the lobby for a final interview with U.S. Embassy staff.

Jim killed time by chatting with a couple from Connecticut. After they tired of talking about the adoption process, they admired the beauty of the main lobby. Huge marble columns complemented the highly polished marble floor that was so shinny, guests could look down and see their own reflection as they walked. To one side of the lobby, a marble spiral staircase led to an expansive open balcony. Jim commented that he thought the Sunway was one of the most beautiful hotels he'd ever stayed at.

When Jim's name was called, Dr. Hendrie's assistant, a strikingly beautiful young woman dressed in a white kimono, insisted on accompanying Jim to care for Brendan during the interview. Based on Brendan's contentment in the car seat, Jim thought the assistance was not needed, but why argue. Within minutes after the interview started, the beautiful young assistant probably wanted to pull her kimono over her face to fashion a breathing mask after Brendan dropped a foul load that would have sent a family of skunks on the run. *Wow! What's hiding in that formula I'm feeding him? This is incredibly embarrassing, but what can I do? At least I don't have to worry about my Mitchum breaking down.*

The Embassy Staff consisted of a pleasant American woman who looked very attractive and professional in a white suit. She had two male assistants, one American and one Cambodian, who both looked foolish to be dressed in black suits. It must have been a hundred degrees outside. The lady greeted Jim, shook his hand, and asked him for help in the pronunciation of his family name. She did all the talking, beginning with chitchat to make Jim feel at ease, even disclosing to him that she too was an adoptive parent with two Cambodian children. Then she began the checklist of questions that Dr. Hendrie had reviewed with all the parents at the previous night's group session. Jim thought it was a good thing that they'd been prepped, and a good thing this lady was very understanding about how tired and stressed out many of the parents were at this stage of the game. She smiled an occasional hint that she was embarrassed to be asking such bureaucratically dim-witted questions.

"Do you intend to take good care of your child?"

"Yes, of course I do," but only *while anyone's watching, that is. The rest of the time I really plan to bat him around the house and neglect him to get even for all the money and grief I've gone through to get the little troublemaker. Do I intend to take good care of my child? What a stupid question.*

At the end of the interview, the lady joined the Brendan Saveth Instant Fan Club by remarking how cute he looked. Jim thanked her for the compliment, for her time, and for trying to make the interview as tolerable as possible. He couldn't wait to get out of that bureaucratic torture chamber and get Brendan changed. He and the woman shook hands again, and he walked briskly to the elevator, trying to hold the car seat slightly behind him so he'd be upwind from the foul trail he was leaving behind. He smiled to himself and thanked God for granting him a sense of humor.

22

Thursday Night, August 3, 2000

o o o o o o o o o o o o o o o o o o o o o o o o o o o o

My name is Brendan Saveth. Tonight I will get my visa for America. Tomorrow, my Daddy will take me home.

After a much-needed diaper change for Brendan and a quick shower and change of clothes for himself, Jim returned to the main lobby where the adoptive parents were gathering prior to a 5:00 pm departure to the American Embassy. There were more than a dozen adoptive parents, most with spouses, and although fatigue was evident on the majority of faces, the group was animated and in high spirits. This was their great moment. Their time had come. All the anticipation, all the months and years of frustration, all the money spent, all the emotional roller coasters, all the prayers and fears were about to become history. They had their babies in their arms, and within the hour, they would have the babies' visas in their hands. Would any other time in their lives be more meaningful, more rewarding?

Artchu pulled up to the Sunway right on schedule, as did most of the drivers for the other parents. Within minutes, a cavalcade of cars turned down the narrow street leading to the embassy compound, and a mad scramble followed for limited parking spaces, but all the drivers somehow managed to squeeze their small autos into available spots. The uniformed, armed guards waved the parents through the high gate and directed the group down a long narrow street within the compound. On one side of the street was residential housing for embassy employees, and on the other side were embassy office buildings. Children played kickball and soccer in the street.

A Cambodian guard at the entrance to the main embassy building collected all their cameras; the parents would need to rely on their memories for this evening's Kodak moments. Passing through a couple of thick, reinforced doors secured by electric locks, the group was herded into a large interior room. The assembly hall had long pews and a wall with a large window made of thick bulletproof glass. A curtain covered a curved section of the window.

As children scampered around and under the pews, parents milled about, chatting about how happy they were to be nearing the end of the long adoptive journey. The lady from Iowa was there alone with her crying baby. Jim speculated facetiously that the husband had either fled the country and his wife, or was back at the hotel hanging himself. The baby cried throughout.

Shortly, the curtain was drawn and revealed another bulletproof movie theatre ticket window with a metal slot and tray for passing through papers. Embassy staff behind the window began calling out names, one at the time. As each name was called and parents walked to the window to receive their baby's visa, the other parents and children in the room broke into a rousing ovation.

Finally, "Pacenka!"

"C'mon Brendan, that's us. Let's go get your visa."

He scooped up his baby and walked quickly to the window, only vaguely aware of the cheering and applause behind him. The lady in the white suit who had interviewed him at the hotel smiled at him and Brendan through the bulletproof glass.

"Congratulations," she said as she passed a large manila envelope through the slot. The envelope had a special seal and warning, "DO NOT OPEN". Inside were the visa and other documents needed to leave Cambodia and to pass through INS screening upon returning to the United States.

As the last person returned from the window with the visa package, the group spontaneously erupted into loud and sustained cheering. Simultaneously, a dozen or more embassy staff came over to stand in front of the large window and they too applauded, though they could be seen but not heard through the bulletproof glass. As they stood at the window, smiling, and nodding approval, Jim thought the scene looked bizarre or surreal. With all the embassy staff pressed against the window, their faces distorted by the thick glass, Jim felt as if the parents and children were specimens being observed by mad scientists studying behavioral responses to the adoption experience. Jim thought he could make out some sad faces among the Embassy staff since many of them thought they were looking at the last batch of American adoptive parents. The moratorium was due to take effect the next day. But bizarre, normal or indefinable, the moment for the parents was one of pure relief, joy and accomplishment. And just as he'd felt when Brendan was placed in his arms, Jim wished Jan could be at his side.

After retrieving their cameras from the guard, the group poured out of the Embassy into the humid, tranquil evening air. They joked and chatted in a festive mood as they walked down the narrow street towards the gate. As they passed the children playing soccer, a misdirected kick sent the ball skidding towards one of the men. He stopped the ball between his feet and playfully kicked it towards one of the other men with the side of his foot. The children squealed with delight and the game was on. The women held the babies while Jim and several men formed an ad hoc team. With parents of the Embassy children sitting on the steps of their homes cheering on their sons and daughters, and with the armed guards nearby looking on in amusement, a ten-minute spirited soccer match ensued. As the American men spontaneously regressed into little boys, the soccer ball provided a common language, while laughter and high fives bridged a cultural chasm several centuries deep. Joy to the world…all the boys and girls…

The ride back to the hotel featured the same route through one of Phnom Penh's more depressing neighborhoods. In high spirits, Jim chose not to see the rundown buildings as he gazed absentmindedly at the passing montage of Third World poverty and squalor. He did notice a pack of joggers, dressed alike and seeming to run in formation, though none too fast in the lingering heat of the day.

"What's with the group of joggers," he inquired of Artchu.

"Police cadets."

"Really?"

"See building over there?" Artchu said, pointing to one of the many rundown buildings on the street, "that is police academy. Cadets live there while in training."

Jim assumed that the motivation for entering the academy must be based on the prospect of steady employment in a poor economy.

Arriving at the Sunway, Jim instructed Artchu to pick him up at 6:45 am the next morning so he could get to the airport early in case there were any complications.

◆　　◆　　◆

Jim had a pre-arranged dinner date in the Sunway restaurant with a woman named Eva, the sister of the wife of one of Jim's boyhood friends. Eva, at fifty-four-years-old, was the personification of the independent, modern American woman. She'd been living in Cambodia for some twenty years, settling there after a successful stint with the Peace Corps in Africa. She was single, possessed dual American and Cambodian citizenships, and was fluent in Khmer.

Jim's friend had arranged the dinner date prior to Jim's departure to Cambodia. Of all things, Eva desired a Harry Potter book. Shipping the book from Massachusetts to Phnom Penh would have cost a small fortune…with no guarantee that Eva would ever receive the book. Jim had enthusiastically agreed to play courier for his friend, thinking it might be handy to have a local contact in Phnom Penh and a link back to his civilized world.

Having been fed before accompanying Jim to dinner, Brendan was as content as ever to sit in his car seat and study Jim and Eva as they chatted. It was as if he was as interested as Jim in what she had to say. And she had plenty to talk about, starting with her position with the Cambodian Department of Agricultural Affairs where she taught economics to Cambodian government employees. She was in a unique position to see the developmental needs of the country. As long as the Cambodian government delayed building an efficient infrastructure, starting with massive road-building projects to crisscross the country, Cambodia was doomed to remain mired in its Third World economy. Without good superhighways to link cities and provinces, economic progress would forever be limited to pockets of modern development in cities such as Phnom Penh. The dichotomy was razor sharp, modern structures and computer-based enterprises like the Sunway and the airport for the minority, but primitive rice paddy farming just a stone's throw away for the majority.

Eva ate native cuisine with chopsticks while Jim chose to enjoy a meal of chicken served over tasty stir-fried vegetables. Jim had joined her in ordering a sweet and sour duck soup, but he declined all her subsequent offers to be daring and to try some of her selections. Jim also joined her in having a beer but he worried about its effect due to his continued state of exhaustion and sleep deprivation. He couldn't afford to crash after dinner because he still had to pack and get ready for his early morning departure.

Jim thoroughly enjoyed the dinner and Eva's company. She gave him a small bracelet to bring back to her sister in Worcester in thanks for the Harry Potter book. He regrettably said goodnight and goodbye to Eva and retreated to his room.

Under Brendan's watchful eye, Jim spent a couple hours packing, repacking and trying to consolidate all his belongings. On the return trip, he would not only be hauling the luggage he'd brought over, but he would also need one arm free to carry Brendan in the car seat. After reaching a point in the consolidation where Jim could find no further possibility for improvement, he changed and fed Brendan and put him to bed.

As Brendan dropped off into almost immediate sleep, Jim helped himself to a Jack Daniels nip from the wet bar, made himself comfortable in the room's large upholstered chair and relaxed. He reflected on his two days in Cambodia, the people he'd met, the moratorium, and his glimpses of life in Phnom Penh. He poured himself a second drink and thought about all he'd been through, looked over at Brendan sleeping so peacefully, and decided easily that it had all been worth the effort. Feeling the effects of the first two drinks, Jim had a third, crawled into bed and prayed that Jack Daniels would tumble him into the full night's sleep he so desperately needed. He went out like a snuffed candle.

23

Friday Morning, August 4, 2000

o o o o o o o o o o o o o o o o o o o o o o o o o o o
My name is Brendan Saveth. Today a big bird will fly me from my past to my future. It will be a long flight, but I will not mind because I take with me a gift from Buddha, acceptance of myself through meditation.

By 2:00 a.m. it was clear that Jack Daniels alone would not be sufficient to guarantee a decent night's sleep through all the noise from outside; it would take knockout pills, soundproof earmuffs, or a room in a different part of the hotel. It wasn't so much the loud voices. It wasn't the banging of metal containers. It wasn't even the gong of the hillside clock, which by now had begun to sound pleasant. It was the music, the loud, piercing, screeching music from the loading dock. *Man, that doesn't even sound like music; it sounds like the world's worst amplifier feedback recorded for use in a torture chamber.* Jim got up and busied himself with sterilizing nipples and preparing bottles of formula for the day ahead. Later, he tried again to sleep.

As daylight began to creep through the window, Jim got up, showered and shaved, and then changed and dressed Brendan before becoming one of the first customers of the day at the breakfast buffet. While Jim was still working on his omelets, Artchu showed up early.

"I have laundry."

"Great. Good job, Artchu. I wanted to wear the Bermuda shorts with all the pockets. They'll come in handy for the trip back."

Artchu accompanied Jim to his room to help with the luggage. When Jim came down to the lobby to check out, he had a large bag of supplies that he left at the front desk to be passed on to the orphanage. He'd ended up with a surplus of baby bottles and nipples, extra bottles of drinking water, extra diapers, and extra baby formula.

During the drive to the airport, Jim gazed out the window, his heart awash in a swirling emotional crosscurrent. As dawn's light stirred Phnom Penh's inhabitants to another day of life...a life of incomprehensible disparities...he saw an old lady on her hands and knees in the gutter, sweeping dirt back into a roadside flowerbox; then, a young girl, a street child, on the sidewalk near the train station, dirty and only half clothed, stretching and yawning to face another day of homeless, childhood hell; an old man with his wife on a dilapidated bicycle, peddling by a Volkswagen dealership sporting shiny new automobiles through large showroom windows; a well-dressed businessman on a loaded $15,000 Kawasaki motorcycle zipping past a disheveled man and his family of four standing beside their broken-down moped.

There were times Jim wanted to speak up, to tell Artchu to stop the car so he could run over and give the little girl or the out-of-luck father a ten-dollar bill. But his mind was numb from lack of sleep and it refused to send a signal to his voice. He argued with himself silently about how such a gift would be received. Would it be with gratitude, or with an attitude of insult? He couldn't decide, couldn't bring himself to ask Artchu for an opinion, and couldn't speak, so he didn't stop. *Home, just get me home.*

After unloading the luggage from the car at the airport, Jim insisted on taking one last photo of Artchu, and then prevailed on a nearby security guard to take a photo of Artchu, Brendan and himself standing together.

"Come on in with me," Jim said.

"Cannot go," Artchu replied, "we must say goodbye here".

"Why not? What's the big deal about going in? I'd like you to come in with me."

"Cannot go. It not allowed."

Jim persisted, "Why not? C'mon, go ask the guard if you can come in with me to help with the luggage and the baby."

Artchu reluctantly went over to the guard. They spoke rapidly in short Khmer sentences as they looked at Jim and Brendan. Artchu came back, grabbed the luggage and accompanied Jim into airport. Things went well at the Cambodian Royal Air ticket counter and Jim was quickly checked in and issued his boarding passes.

Several other adoptive parents arrived and checked in for their flights. Jim stood around with them making small talk; all were eager to get on with the journey home. When another of the group, a man from Newburyport, Massachusetts came over from the ticket counter and announced that their plane was pulling up to a gate, it was time to say goodbye to Artchu.

"I want to thank you for everything, Artchu, for all your help. You've been wonderful to me and Brendan."

"You tell him about me when he older?"

"You bet. I'll tell Brendan about 'Uncle Artchu' and how good he was for us."

They shook hands, hugged as warmly as men can hug, and went their separate ways.

Jim's next hurdle was the immigration desk. He'd already completed a required form and passed it to a lady behind the counter. In less than pleasant tones, she told Jim that he needed an additional form completed for Brendan. Jim took the form and went off to the side to fill it out. When he returned to her, she told him the form was incorrect, and without trying to be helpful, sent him off to do it right. After doing his best to complete the form properly, Jim decided to try an end run and walked up to a man at the far end of the counter while the lady was pre-occupied giving someone else a hard time.

The man took the forms, looked at them, and looked back at Jim with a wry smile. He left his booth and walked down to the end of the counter and showed Jim's form to the lady. She looked over at Jim and gave him a "what're you trying to pull" smirk. After a brief exchange between the two bureaucrats, the man came back and gave Jim a friendly nod.

"I take care of this. You not have to go back to her."

"Oh, thank you, thanks very much," Jim said, playing dumb. "I didn't know I was supposed to go back to her."

"All set," he said as he sent Jim on his way.

Shortly after reaching the gate area, an announcement came over the speaker system stating that the plane had arrived and boarding would soon begin. When the loading process began, handicapped passengers and passengers with infants and young children were invited to board ahead of other passengers. As Jim handed over his and Brendan's boarding passes, the attendant hesitated, looked at a small screen and told Jim he needed to pay another twenty dollars.

"You need another twenty dollars?"

"Yes, for your child's seat."

"For his seat?"

"Yes. There's a twenty-dollar surcharge for each occupied seat. Yours has been paid but not your child's. Since he has his own seat, I must collect another twenty dollars."

People in line behind Jim began to groan and mumble about the delay and about the absurdity of the ambiguous fee for the child's seat. Jim fumbled as quickly as he could into his pockets and found a twenty-dollar bill. Cleared for passage, Jim walked through the doors onto the warm tarmac that was already radiating heat from the bright morning sun.

There were stairs leading to entrance doors at the front and at the middle of the plane. Since Jim's seats were in the first row behind the small first class section, he was directed to the front door. As he buckled Brendan's car seat and settled in for the relatively short flight from

Phnom Penh to Hong Kong, Jim naturally fell into conversation with the lady sitting beside him, a short, pudgy, older American woman carrying her adopted baby. She was from Iowa, and though she was at least sixty years old and a single parent, she was bringing home her second Cambodian child in as many years.

They chatted about the adoption experience and made idle conversation while awaiting takeoff. The more they talked, the less friendly she seemed. She made many "off the wall" comments and was extremely opinionated about everything and everybody. Jim was glad it was going to be a relatively short flight.

As is often the case during takeoffs, much of the conversation among the passengers trailed off dramatically, making the passenger cabin very quiet as everyone listened to the powerful jet engines roar their challenge to the laws of gravity. Either the runway was quite short or the pilot was something of a cowboy as passengers were flattened against the backs of their seats in a very fast and steep takeoff. The rifle-shot accent to high altitude created more than the usual pressure in the cabin and immediately caused some of the babies with sensitive ears to begin crying. Brendan blew out his flip-flop.

Jim had been attempting to give Brendan a bottle to suck on as a distraction to the takeoff. With the extreme pressure created by the plane rocketing to high altitude, Brendan rejected the nipple and joined the chorus of crying babies, simultaneously exploding a huge bowel movement into his diaper. When the plane began to level off, Jim made the mistake of unbuckling Brendan and taking him into his arms to try to comfort him from the painful ear pressure. A killer load, with the color of pea soup and the stench of rotting fish, oozed from the sides of the diaper, smearing Jim's hands and arms and dribbling onto his just-back-from-the-laundry Bermudas.

As Jim attempted to hold Brendan with one arm while unfastening his seat belt, the two men in the adjacent seats couldn't resist leaning over to offer tongue-in-cheek comments.

"Looks like you've got an armful there," said one of the men.

"The takeoff made him poop," Jim replied red-faced.

"Whew," the other said wrinkling his nose, "you're telling us?"

"Sorry about that."

"Hey, like they say, shit happens," the man said, trying to be a little sympathetic to Jim's plight.

Seeing Jim waiting patiently in the aisle for one of the occupied lavatories in the coach section of the plane, and wanting to expedite Jim's need to deal with the stench permeating the entire front of the plane, an attendant quickly told Jim it would be okay for him to use one of the first class toilets to change Brendan. Jim was pleased with the offer because he knew the first class lavatory would be much larger than in coach, making it easier to clean and change Brendan.

Jim stripped Brendan, trying to avoid breathing too deeply. The sink was large enough to enable him to hand bathe the small infant. After first trying to wash Brendan's tee shirt, Jim just tossed it into the trash along with the diaper. Digging into his large diaper bag, Jim became more appreciative than ever of Jan's comprehensive planning and packing assistance since she had stashed extra clothes for contingencies such as he now faced. After cleaning himself and his Bermudas as best he could and making Brendan look and smell like the cute bundle of joy he was, Jim sprayed the air liberally with the sanitizer provided in the first class lavatory, dabbed some men's fragrance on himself, and returned to his seat feeling acceptable to the world again. The remainder of the flight was uneventful.

As the plane circled to land in Hong Kong, Jim thought the view was beautiful and surprising. Despite rain splattering against the window, he could see many fishing boats in the harbor just as he imagined he would, but he hadn't expected to see snow-capped mountains nearby. After the searing heat of Cambodia, seeing the snow in the distance and the rain on the window while sitting in a super-chilled air-conditioned plane, Jim suddenly felt like it was winter. His senses were instantly readjusted when he stepped off the plane into the warm Hong Kong air.

While passing through Customs, Jim discovered that the gate for his next flight on China Air was at the opposite end of the air terminal. Thinking he had to rush to make the connecting flight, Jim made a mad dash to China Air only to discover that he had an hour to spare before boarding.

While killing time for the next flight, Jim looked around the waiting room and saw only a portion of the adoptive parents who had been on his Royal Air flight to Hong Kong. Apparently, some of the others were either taking a different airline back to the United States, or they were on different China Air flights. Though he was curious about what airline or flights they had, he wasn't about to mess with his itinerary that had him boarding a China Air flight that would make only a brief stopover in Taipei before continuing on to Los Angeles. There, he would connect with a United Airlines flight to Boston.

He thought about giving Jan a call to tell her he was already in Hong Kong and about to depart for Taipei, but she'd be sleeping and he decided there was no point in waking her. Although it was Friday noon for him, it was midnight on Thursday for Jan.

Soon, he was on the jumbo jet, strapping Brendan's car seat into the plane's seat. This leg of his journey home, from Hong Kong to Taipei, would be the shortest of the four flights home. It would be only a couple hours, something equivalent to a Boston to Chicago flight.

The Air China jet was a spacious wide body type plane with plenty of legroom between the rows of seats. Every time Jim walked the aisles of the cavernous aircraft, he found himself in awe of the size of the plane. Boeing was fond of boasting about the fact that at 150 feet, the 747's economy section alone was longer than the length of the Wright Brother's first flight at Kitty Hawk. The only complaint Jim had was that the air conditioning system kept the plane extremely cool, almost cold. Jim shut the air vents above his and Brendan's seat, but it made no difference. He kept Brendan covered with a blanket and the relatively short flight to Taipei was soon over.

Jim thought the Taipei airport looked spectacular as they flew in, with bright green lights outlining the runways. The 727 had a video camera on the nose of the plane that allowed passengers to have a pilot's view of the landing on the passenger TV screens. The sight of a plane taking off directly ahead of his plane as they landed fascinated Jim but gave him pause about the need for precise timing by the air controllers. Moments later, as the plane taxied to a gate, he and the passengers on his side of the plane were also treated to the sight of the mangled remains of a jet that had suffered a landing collision with another plane just a couple weeks earlier. *I could do without seeing that just now!*

The stopover in Taipei was a brief one, just long enough to fill the plane to capacity with passengers and fuel for the long flight to Los Angeles. Jim debated getting off the plane to walk and stretch for a few minutes, but the idea seemed like more bother than it was worth, so he opted to stay put as the new passengers began boarding almost immediately. The process seemed to move quickly, and before long, the China Air 747 jumbo jet was taxiing down the runway with a full capacity of crew and passengers totaling over five hundred.

Jim settled in and tried not to think about the length of this part of the journey, more than thirteen hours. He tried to focus on the positive thought that he was homeward bound. Additionally, there were many distractions during the first part of the flight. Passengers were pampered with drinks and food and warm, moist towels after meals. Jim enjoyed his chicken teriyaki with rice, complete with tea and fortune cookie.

Sitting in a nearby row, among new passengers who boarded in Taipei, was an adoptive couple bringing home a baby from China. They were young and appeared nervous. Jim didn't know if they had other children, but they appeared to be quite ill at ease and awkward with the baby. And the baby was a crier. On one occasion, while Jim was standing in the aisle to stretch, he tried to be helpful by telling the mother that perhaps the baby was cold from the air conditioning on the plane. He suggested that she try putting a blanket over the baby as he had done with Brendan. She chose to ignore the suggestion. The baby chose to cry intermittently for thirteen hours.

The hours dragged on as the aircraft streaked through the black night at nearly 600 miles per hour. Just as he had hoped that his plane didn't go down in the Himalayas on the way to Cambodia, Jim now prayed that the plane didn't go down while cruising over the Pacific. *How the hell can this huge thing stay up in the air for thirteen hours? How much fuel must this thing need to do that. And how does this thing even stay up in the air with all that weight plus the five hundred of us with tons of luggage? I hope the mechanics checked out those jet engines real good before we took off.*

By the time Jim got tired enough to sleep, Brendan was back wide-awake and in the mood for attention. Jim took him out of his car seat and entertained him for a while before sitting him in his lap. Predictably, it wasn't long before Jim found himself beginning to nod off. He caught himself slipping into that longed-for abyss and snapped his head back with eyes wide open. Two China Air attendants were standing in the aisle beside him, watching, waiting to catch Brendan. Jim smiled sheepishly, thanked them for their vigilance and concern, and strapped Brendan back into the car seat. By the time they approached Los Angeles, Jim had managed to snatch only an hour or two of sleep along the way. He was starting to get used to functioning in a zombie state.

Jim checked his watch as the pilot banked the plane for the landing. He figured it would be nearly 3:00 p.m. by the time he was off the plane. His United Airlines flight was scheduled to depart for Boston at 3:30. *I'm going to have to get through Customs and Immigration and then boogie from the China Air terminal to United in thirty minutes. This ain't gonna be easy.*

Jim's seat on the flight from Taipei was about a third of the way back from the front of the plane and he waited impatiently for the passengers in the rows ahead of him to move off the plane. Once off, Jim hustled as best he could to pass ahead of slow-walking passengers to get closer to the front of the pack. He was able to zip through Immigration quickly, turning in his sealed visa packet and receiving signed documents that would allow him later to obtain a Social Security number and "Green Card" for Brendan.

With his carry-on backpack and diaper bag in one hand and Brendan snuggled in his car seat in the other, Jim dashed to the baggage claim conveyors. As the minutes ticked away, Jim had no choice but to wait in agonized frustration for luggage to appear. When it did, Jim and the other passengers watched in disbelief as a female airport worker began grabbing luggage off the long conveyor and throwing it roughly to the floor. The beefy, macho female attendant with crew cut hair and a nose ring wore a scowl that screamed, "I just love how much I hate my job." She ignored the murmurs and grumbling from nearby passengers about her treatment of their luggage. As she continued to slam the bags to the floor, one female passenger walked over to confront her.

"Hey, take it easy with our luggage."

"Get lost," the worker replied while grabbing and tossing more bags in a heap.

The passenger walked over to a nearby security guard and complained. The security guard shrugged his shoulders and said there was nothing he could do about it. A male passenger approached the guard with the same results and demanded that the guard call a supervisor. Meanwhile, the worker kept ignoring all protests as she grabbed and threw as many bags as she could. Some passengers tried to spot their luggage as it started down the conveyor and then run over to grab it before it reached the demented baggage handler. Jim followed suit and did an end run around her when he spied his bags coming down.

When he reached Customs, he was pleasantly surprised to find that he and the adoptive parents were receiving special treatment by being expedited through a separate line set up for pilots and airline attendants. After breezing through that hurdle with a quick declaration of his Phnom Penh souvenirs, Jim asked for directions to the United Airlines terminal and discovered it was quite some distance from the international terminals. He went outside, found an abandoned luggage cart, stacked his bags with Brendan on top, and began to push the cart in a run down the sidewalk. Shouting "sorry" or "excuse me" to travelers who dived out of his way, Jim pulled up breathless and dripping with sweat at a United Airlines customer service counter at 3:30 p.m. There were two women and a man behind the counter.

"I'm here to catch the 3:30 flight to Boston" Jim blurted hopefully.

"It's left the gate," the male agent said matter-of-factly.

"Are you sure? Can you check to make sure," Jim pleaded.

"It's left the gate," the agent repeated coldly, looking at his watch.

"C'mon, can you check for me. If it hasn't left you could ask them to hold it for another couple minutes till I run over there. Just call over there, please."

"It's out of the gate and on the runway by now, waiting for takeoff."

"Look, I've just traveled halfway around the world today with this little guy I adopted. I just want to get home. Can't you check? Maybe it was delayed a few minutes at the gate."

The man was unmoved by Jim's pleas, refused to call the gate, and insisted that the plane had left the gate.

"Okay, just tell me what gate it was leaving from."

"Fifty-four. You need to go that way and up one level," he said flatly, pointing out the direction.

Jim took off with his cart in a dead run, spotted an elevator, and ran to it. When the door opened, he discovered that another passenger with a cart already filled the elevator. Jim scooped up his bags and Brendan, abandoned the cart, and bounded up the escalator. He ran to the passageway to Gate 54 only to find the way blocked by a security-screening portal.

"You can't come through here with that big bag. It won't fit through the x-ray machine. You're only supposed to be coming through here with carry-on luggage."

"I'm trying to see if my plane left the gate yet. How can I do that?

"We'll, you can leave your luggage here and go to the gate."

Jim knew defeat when it whacked him over the head. The plane most likely had left the gate by now anyway. The situation was hopeless. He'd need to go back to the United counter and rebook for a later flight. Although he was frustrated with missing the plane, it was not a surprise. When he and Jan had made the flight arrangements, they understood that catching the mid-afternoon United flight to Boston would be a long shot and would only be possible if the China Air flight from Taipei arrived early, or if the United flight departed late. His frustration came from having come so close to making the flight. Less delay at the baggage claim area might have allowed him to make the connection.

Jim returned to the United ticket counter to find that long queues had developed for all the agents. He spotted some of the other Massachusetts adoptive parents milling around and went over to talk with them.

"We're giving up the idea of trying to make it back home today. We're going to get a room at a hotel and get out in the morning," one of the weary parents said. Although their watches had gained twelve hours through the magic of flying east through the international dateline, the reality was that they had been "on the road" for over twenty-fours hours since they'd left Phnom Penh. They were dragging.

"How come?" Jim asked, not understanding why they wouldn't be just as desperate as he was to get home.

"No way you can get home today. From what we hear, all the flights to Boston are filled. The only choice is a red-eye overnight, or wait till morning."

"No kidding?"

"No kidding. A hotel bed sounds more appealing right now than a six or seven-hour wait in airport chairs to catch the red-eye. We've had it."

"Ditto. Man, a shower and a bed sound awfully tempting right now, but I just want to get home."

The parents went off in search of a hotel, leaving Jim looking at the long queues for the United ticket counters.

24

Friday Afternoon, August 4, 2000

My name is Kimberly and I'm so excited! Mommy says Daddy will be home tomorrow with Brendan. I can't wait! I look at his picture a lot...he's so cute!

Unbeknown to Jim, Jan's Friday had begun with another emotional storm. She had been looking forward to this day all week but dreading it at the same time. She wanted Jim home with the baby, but after all the problems with the flights over to Cambodia, she was worried about the return flight arrangements. The last thing she needed that morning was a confusing call from a China Air representative.

"Hello."

"Hello, dis missis Pisinka?"

"Yes?"

"Dis China Air. Is you husband on plane?"

"What"

"You husband on plane?"

"You tell me. What do you mean is he on the plane? Is something wrong?"

"You husband on plane?"

"Yes, yes, he's supposed to be. What's wrong? What's happened to the plane?" Jan said in a growing panic, thinking her darkest fears. *Jim went over there to create a family, but instead, I'm going to end up being a widow with one child.*

The conversation went nowhere. The China Agent spoke such broken English that Jan could not begin to understand why she was being called, why the lady wanted to know if Jim was on the plane. The more panic the agent heard in Jan's voice, the faster she spoke in incomprehensible broken English. Jan said goodbye, hung up, and immediately called China Air. The supervisor she reached had no idea why Jan received the call she described and said she'd look into the matter immediately.

Jan called her sister and told her about the strange call and the follow-up call she'd made to China Air. Jan's sister told her to relax and she'd do some research over the Internet to see if she could learn anything else. Later, she called Jan back to tell her that there was no reported plane crash of a commercial airliner anywhere in the world. Jan should stop worrying about the possibility.

Jan appreciated her sister's reassuring words, but she could not stop worrying. An eternity of an hour later, the supervisor from China Air called Jan with an explanation for the earlier call. A new employee, still in training, who had been instructed to call the day before to confirm that Jim planned to be on the return flight, had erroneously made the call. Such a follow-up contact was a routine procedure for any passenger like Jim who had missed the flight over to Cambodia. The trainee, however, should never have made the call when she did. The supervisor apologized for the erroneous call and Jan felt better…but her nerves were still frazzled.

Doing her best to remain positive, Jan spent the afternoon running last minute errands and doing chores left undone during the hectic week. She also spent time making final preparations for Brendan's room. The busy work helped, but as the day wore on without any word concerning Jim's whereabouts, she couldn't stop the building edginess that ate at her insides. As evening began to draw the sun down behind the western hills, she began to pace nervously in anticipation of a call from Jim. *Where is he? He should have called by now. It's after three-thirty in LA. He was supposed to call. If he made the afternoon connection, he's back in the air, due in Boston around 11:30 p.m. Do I just go to Boston tonight figuring he'll be there? Where is he?*

◆   ◆   ◆

Jim felt too exhausted and frustrated to stand in line at the back of the ever-lengthening queue. He looked around for a roving United Airlines customer service agent, spotted one, and went over to plead his case. She listened sympathetically to Jim's plight, saw the weariness in his face, heard the desperation in his voice, and probably smelled the drying perspiration from his failed attempt to make the 3:30 pm connection to Boston.

"Follow me," the agent said, leading Jim away from the huge crowd of waiting travelers and bringing him to an agent at the far end of the counter area. She lined Jim up behind a small number of people waiting patiently at a special counter set up by United for passengers traveling with their pets. She went over and said something to the ticket agent, came back towards Jim, gave him a wink with a thumbs up sign, and went back to her duties with the multitudes at the main counter. Jim felt a bit out of place, but he liked the idea of having only a handful of passengers ahead of him instead of hundreds. So he proudly held his smiling Brendan as he stood behind others holding barking poodles, meowing Tiger cats, and screeching cockatoos.

The ticket agent confirmed the unwanted news he'd heard from the other parents; there was no other available seat on a United flight to Boston until 10:30 pm. As a courtesy, she gamely tried to find him a flight on any other airline, but the best she could find was a late afternoon flight with a long layover in Las Vegas that would result in Jim reaching Boston only about an hour earlier than the non-stop 10:30 p.m. United flight. Jim thanked her for trying but opted for the ten-thirty red-eye. She checked his large Pullman and issued his tickets. He set off to find a phone.

In August 2000, cell phone mania had not yet enslaved America and Jim found all the public pay phones fully utilized. Frustration and hunger caused him to temporarily abandon his quest for an available telephone in favor of food. After a quick bite to eat, he set off again in search of an available pay phone.

◆ ◆ ◆

Judy, one of Jan's sisters telephoned almost every hour on the hour to ask if Jim had called. With Kimberly still not fully recovered from her summer virus, the plan was for the sister to come over to baby-sit, while her husband, a former part-time limo driver, drove to Boston with Jan to pick up Jim and Brendan. The plan was on hold.

Another of Jan's sisters, Joanne, the sister who had done the Internet research earlier in the day to help assure Jan that there were no commercial airline crashes to worry about, called around 8:30 p.m.

"Have you heard from him yet?"

"No."

"What're you going to do about Logan? You still going down there tonight?"

"I don't know. I really don't know what to do."

"Hey, are you okay?"

"I'm okay," Jan answered unconvincingly.

"Are you sure? Do you need someone with you?"

"Yah, I think I do."

They talked a while longer and decided it made sense for Jan to call Judy, who lived the closest to Jan, to ask her to come over without waiting to hear from Jim. Jan called Judy who readily agreed to come over the house with her husband. They'd keep Jan company until she heard from Jim, and Judy would plan on sleeping over anyway. They arrived at Jan's home around 9:00 p.m., EST, to learn with dismay that Jim had still not been heard from.

◆   ◆   ◆

It was close to 6:30 p.m. west coast time when Jim found an available pay phone, but Murphy's Law prevailed once again as his AT&T calling card kept getting rejected by the AT&T phone. He finally got an operator's help.

"Jan."

"Where are you?" Jan demanded to know with more frustration and anger than love in her voice. She'd been worrying about him for more than twelve hours, since the bizarre call from the China Air woman that morning.

"L.A., I'm in Los Angeles," Jim answered, laughing at the motherly scolding he heard in the tone of her three simple words.

"I've been going nuts all day waiting to hear from you."

"I know, I know, but it was too early to call you when I was in Hong Kong and Taipei, and I've been going nuts here trying to get a flight from LA to Boston."

"I'm so relieved to hear your voice and know that you're back in our country."

He told her about the other parents crashing for the night at a local hotel and about his decision to hang around the airport and take the red-eye home. He gave her the departure and arrival schedule along with the flight number.

"You might as well get yourself a good night's sleep," he said.

"Oh sure, like there's a chance of that," Jan replied, knowing she'd be getting to bed late, be up during the night giving Kimberly medication, and then getting up around 4:30 a.m. to head for Logan Airport.

Jim spent the next few hours wandering around the Los Angeles airport, pushing an uncomplaining Brendan around on a luggage cart. He killed some time people watching, shopping in the airport stores for souvenirs to bring home, watching a TV in a pizza shop and talking to Brendan, who smiled at the attention. The smile had captured Jim's heart from the very first meeting, and whenever Jim felt himself getting too down or frustrated, he talked to his "Big Guy" and elicited the smile. It was like a diabetic getting a needed surge of sugar.

Sometime during the evening, Jim spent almost an hour creating a bit of a scene in one of the men's restrooms. He was no longer flying first class with access to Thai Air Royal Lounges. He was back in America flying coach, and there wasn't even a changing station in the men's restroom. He made due at one end of the sink counter.

Brendan needed a diaper change and some cleaning up. Jim ignored the side-glances of the Hispanic restroom attendant along with the looks of incredulity or disgust from some macho executives in their tailored suits who had probably never changed a diaper in their lives. He gave Brendan a sponge bath as best he could considering the automatic shutoff faucets. Brendan didn't mind the lack of privacy or Spartan amenities. He smiled winningly at all who stared at him, and seemed fascinated by his reflection in the large wall mirror behind the sink.

Jim dressed Brendan in a clean blue outfit and set him up in his car seat with a bottle of formula. With a content Brendan at his side, Jim dug out his toiletry kit and gave himself the luxury of a shave, something he needed badly by now. After all, today was really yesterday. He retrieved a clean shirt from his carry-on bag, and despite having to remain in the Bermuda shorts soiled by Brendan in the takeoff from Phnom Penh, Jim exited the restroom feeling much better about himself.

After a few hours, Jim grew tired of wandering the airport and making contributions to the pestering solicitors for the needy "brothers" of Los Angeles. He found his way to the gate area for his United flight to Boston and hunkered down for the duration. As the night wore on, the waiting area filled to capacity and Jim was glad that he had arrived early.

Since the departure was scheduled for ten-thirty, Jim expected to see a plane pulling in to the gate area by at least ten o'clock. Nothing doing. Jim kept shooting glances through the large floor to ceiling windows only to keep seeing an empty gate. By twenty past ten, Jim and other passengers were besieging the United agents at the gate desk with questions about the flight. The answer was always the same: the plane was en route. It finally showed up about ten minutes after its scheduled departure.

Jim was pleased to be able to be among the first allowed to board. He was less than pleased when he discovered his seat was in the middle of the very last row, sandwiched between two Asian women. He had never been in a tighter seat. *It's gonna be a long five and a half hours. Well, at least I won't have to worry about falling out of my seat. Oh what the hell, I'm almost home.*

◆ ◆ ◆

While Jim had been wandering around the LA airport, Jan sat up late with her sister and wandered through reflections about the long, torturous, emotional adoption saga that had led to this night. They chatted until 1:30 in the morning. The final thought of the night was Judy's amazement with Brendan's good fortune; how, of all the millions of orphaned children throughout the many undeveloped countries of the world, this one baby was having the good fortune to be plucked from a guaranteed hellish life in a primitive village, flown halfway around the world to an affluent America, and welcomed into the loving arms of parents taking a leap of faith on the basis of a baby picture. Surely, Judy concluded, this was one lucky baby.

25

Saturday, August 5, 2000

○ ○

My name is Kimberly and I'm really, really happy this morning because today my daddy is coming home from Cambodia with my new baby brother.

After what amounted to little more than a nap, Jan was up at 3:00 a.m. to give Kimberly her medication, and by 4:30, she was up and preparing to leave for Boston. Jim's red-eye was due in at 6:30. Even though the traffic should be insignificant so early in the morning, Jan wanted to leave by 5:00. Delays in getting to Logan Airport had a way of happening at any time of the day; if it wasn't traffic, it could be a detour, or construction, or tunnel maintenance, or an accident, or whatever.

While Jim's plane cruised uneventfully four miles high over New York and Connecticut toward the morning fireball on the horizon, Jan and her brother-in-law zipped along quiet Massachusetts highways toward the same beautiful sunrise, both destined for a Logan Airport that was just beginning to work itself into another day's frenzy. Jan was extremely happy that her brother-in-law had offered to drive her to Logan. Boston was in the midst of its massive "Big Dig" construction project for the Central Artery, the largest highway construction project in US history. And Logan was undergoing its perpetual reconstruction. Given her exhaustion and state of mind, she was sure that she'd have made wrong turns to access the tunnels to Logan, or become lost in the airport's serpentine maze of ramps, never reaching the United terminal on time, even with the early start from home.

◆   ◆   ◆

Jim desperately wanted to sleep on the flight from LA but a frisky Brendan was in the mood for playing and attention, not much sleep. During Brendan's restful periods, Jim had time for quiet contemplation while most passengers slept. Early on, after some limited conversation with one of the Asian passengers beside him, Jim's mind began an automatic replay of his improbable journey. Vivid memories with excruciating details of his nightmare journey to Cambodia paraded by but he willed them away with superimposed images of a smiling Brendan. From beginning to end, he felt he'd lived through an incredible odyssey, something he never could have imagined for himself before he started out. And though the journey was near its end, the adventure of life that he held in his arms was just beginning.

The hours dragged on as the minutes drifted slowly away in the plane's jet stream. Unlike the whisper-quiet flight in the well-insulated, upper level Royal Class cabin on Thai Air, there was no escape in his rear seat from the loud, wearisome drone of the jet engines on the United flight. It added to his general fatigue, and despite an infusion of homeward-bound adrenalin, he felt barely functional. Instead of feeling alert and excited as he approached his destination, he felt dazed and listless. It had now been over thirty-seven hours since he'd left the Sunway Hotel in Phnom Penh...and that was following another night of only three or four hours sleep. Jim's energy tank was running on empty, determination his only backup fuel.

The plane arrived in Boston at 7:00 a.m., a half-hour late. When it taxied to a stop at its assigned gate, passengers eagerly unsnapped their seatbelts and jumped into the aisle to retrieve their carry-on luggage from overhead compartments. Not Jim. There was no need to hurry up and wait. Stuck in the last row of seats on the plane, he knew it would take forever before he'd be able to get off, and being a gentleman, he'd be dead last because he'd allow the Asian ladies to go before him.

Jan waited anxiously in the corridor watching the colorful stream of humanity file past. Her eyes darted from passenger to passenger looking for Jim. She had no way of knowing that he was in the last seat. By the time the stream of disembarking passengers from Jim's plane had slowed to a trickle...even the pilots had walked by...Jan was starting to panic. *Did he miss this flight too? He would have called, wouldn't he? Where is he? What's happened to him now? Maybe we missed his call. My god, where is he?*

Just when it seemed that all passengers had exited the plane, along straggled Jim...dead last...walking...as if...he was dead...to the world. As he approached, the moment became as awkward as their first date. The week of tension, fear and uncertainty had drained them both, and they stood shakily for a moment at arm's length, seeing each other through exhausted eyes, looking like two heavyweight fighters unable to move after the last bell because they had beaten themselves silly.

After years on the adoption roller coaster, after months of emotional, physical and financial outlays, after a sleepless week of round-the-clock uncertainty and excruciating tension, the moment should have been golden. There should have been bands playing, cheering crowds, exploding fireworks, and formations of jets streaking a salute overhead. There should have been unbridled joy and incredible exuberance. Instead, they faced each other like strangers in self-conscious silence.

Jan felt numb and confused, lost in sea of thoughts. She knew she was extremely relieved to see Jim back home, safe and sound and successfully returning with the baby they had labored so hard to obtain. She had long imagined this magic moment and it had danced in her mind like a Disney fairytale with a storybook ending. But inexplicably, she felt disappointment rather than elation. The messed-up flight plans had made it impossible for a family gathering to be at the airport to share the moment and to cheer and hug their returning hero. The early morning homecoming seemed lonely and sad.

And Brendan. Here at last was Brendan, in the flesh, not a photo. Jan found herself mesmerized by the site of him; how beautiful he was, how his eyes were so bright and expressive. She thought about what must be going through his mind with all that he'd seen during the forty-eight hours since the nanny had passed him off to Jim at the orphanage. Whisked halfway around the world. So many new faces and places.

To Jim, Jan seemed to be in shock, and her blank expression and unresponsiveness fueled Jim's state of exhaustion and feeling of emptiness with the anticlimax of a mission accomplished. He put everything down and gave Jan a hug and a kiss. Then he lifted Brendan out of the car seat and handed him to Jan, breaking the tongue-tied silence with a simple, "Here's your son."

Jan held Brendan, still paralyzed by a mind trying to process a flood of emotions and thoughts simultaneously. She even found herself feeling inept with how she was holding Brendan. *My god, this is absurd! Have I forgotten how to hold a baby? What is wrong with me?* She finally looked at Jim and mumbled, "You did it. We did it."

After Jan's brother-in-law snapped some pictures, Jim said, "Okay, get me to a Dunkin' Donuts. They didn't serve any food on the red-eye. I'm starved."

They found a Dunkin' in the terminal and Jim devoured a huge glazed cinnamon roll with coffee while Jan tuned herself back into reality and tried not to comment on how bad both Jim and Brendan stunk. It was a unique odor and not pleasant at all. Later, when she delicately brought the subject up for discussion, Jim was oblivious to the stench and surmised it may have been an unwanted souvenir from having the laundry done in Phnom Penh. Given what he'd been through during the past week while circling the globe, he was not the least bit concerned about how he smelled.

An hour and a half later, when they pulled into the driveway of their home, Jim thought the house never looked so beautiful. The front door flew open and Kimberly ran out onto the porch. Jim walked over to her and placed a smiling Brendan down in front of her.

"Here's your little brother."

Kimberly, usually a bubbly chatterbox with a thousand questions or opinions, stood in awed silence, staring at Brendan. Just as Jan had trouble at the airport believing what she was seeing, that Jim was really back, Kimberly seemed to have trouble believing that she was really seeing her new little brother. Perhaps she'd had so many disappointments when past adoptions had fallen through, she was trying to make it sink in that this was for real, or perhaps she was just trying to compare the reality of Brendan with the image of him she had in her mind from the baby pictures they had of Brendan. Or perhaps it was simply that she was still running a temp of a hundred and one. Whatever the reason, mile-a-minute talker Kimberly was speechless.

Jim sat on the porch steps, watching it all as if it was an out of body experience…feeling as if his six-day round-the-world odyssey had all been a dream. He had trouble believing that he'd managed to overcome all the setbacks…that he was home…that he had returned with their adopted child…that he and Jan finally had their family.

After a while, they went inside. Jim dragged himself to his home sweet home bed and tried unsuccessfully to take a nap. Kimberly played house with her dolls, telling each one about her new little brother. Jan took all the clothes that Jim and Brendan came back with and began trying to boil them clean. Brendan immediately fell into a peaceful slumber in his new crib.

26

Sunday, August 6, 2000

○ ○

My name is Kimberly and today, me and my little brother Brendan are going to my auntie's birthday party.

The day after Jim's return from Cambodia, there was a surprise fiftieth birthday party for one of Jan's sisters. Jan and Jim were understandably a bit slow in getting themselves together on Jim's first day back but they still wanted to go to the party. They both had managed a decent night's sleep, and though still emotionally and physically drained, they felt much better. It was good they wouldn't discover for another day that Brendan had contracted a terrible head and chest cold on the long flight home. It was really good that they didn't know that they would spend the coming week seeing doctors and visiting hospitals to have Brendan tested to be sure that what he had was a cold, not tuberculosis. And it was especially good that they didn't see how sick all of them would become in the coming weeks and months and how Jan's cold would develop into pneumonia. It was just good that they felt happy on this day and made it to the party.

When they arrived, they didn't make it five feet from their car before everyone poured out of the house, rushing to envelop them with a flood of warm greetings, making Jan and Jim feel the way they expected to feel the day before at the airport. The friends and relatives had all been part of the "Where In The World Is Jim?" network for the past six days, and many couldn't hide tears of joy as they nearly hugged him to death. But most of all, they wanted to ogle and fuss over the smiling star of the day, Brendan Saveth, newest member of the family.

27

November 2000

○ ○

My name is Julie Anne Pacenka. My parents don't know it yet, but I will be born in August 2001. I will have a terrific big sister, Kimberly, and a cute big brother, Brendan. I am so lucky.

"Jim, you won't believe this…I think I'm pregnant!"

Postscript

In the early 1990's, the Immigration and Naturalization Service (INS) annually issued approximately 60 immigrant visas to Cambodian orphans coming to the United States. By the time the INS began talking about a Cambodian adoption moratorium in 2000 because of questions with Cambodian government processes, the volume of American visas issued to Cambodian orphans had increased one thousand percent to 600 annually.

As luck would have it, Jim's nail-biting race against the moratorium clock was timely. The early August 2000 implementation of the INS moratorium on Cambodian adoptions, though temporary, led to a full suspension of adoption visa processing on December 21, 2001...leaving some 400 frustrated American families in an adoption limbo. Continuing investigations by the INS during 2002 and 2003 eventually led to the conviction of one adoption facilitator during 2004 on charges of visa fraud and money laundering.

Although the suspension remains in effect at the time of this writing (October 2005), the INS has seen fit to grant a limited number of Cambodian orphan visas for "humanitarian" reasons, the most notorious being the one that produced a toddler for film star Angelina Jolie in the summer of 2002. The INS is refusing to lift the suspension of Cambodian adoptions until the Cambodian Government makes legislative and procedural changes.

Meanwhile, the INS has continued to issue immigrant visas by the tens of thousands for orphans from all over the world, especially Russia and China. The issuance of immigrant visas for orphans from those two countries has skyrocketed, accounting for almost 13,000 out of the 22,884 international adoptions by U.S. parents during 2004.

978-0-595-37474-8
0-595-37474-3